This Can't Be The End

Harper Rae James

Dedication

To Mama, Nik, Lyss, Brooke, and Linds, and all women who stand together, support one another, and uplift each others' dreams:
Keep Killin' It!

Trigger Warning

Playlist

FOR AN IMMERSIVE EXPERIENCE, here is a Spotify playlist.

Happy Reading,
Harper Rae

Prologue

Today, March 1st

People say when you die, your entire life flashes before your eyes. Every time I've heard that I've always imagined it being like a slow-motion black-and-white snapshot of core memories flashing at the speed of light. I imagine it in a montage, all at once, only truly focused on the most important parts. Right now I wonder, how anyone really knows, because as I stare down at the love of my life, my lifeline, the one person who holds me together, it doesn't look like anything is happening in her head at all.

What I do know is what happens when you are not the one dying, but breaking apart at the seams, staring at the person you love more than life itself, bleeding out on the sidewalk, held tight in your arms. Everything is numb, I can't think straight, or catch my breath because my heart feels like it's about to pound out of my chest. But more than anything, I wish I could trade places with her.

As I hold Ana's limp body on the corner of her street, exactly 63 steps from her front door, 63 steps I counted as I ran to get her phone to call 911 because mine was dead, all I see is her face. As I stare at her perfect face, tan skin, naturally cherry lips, and the slightest peek of dark circles under her eyes I have memorized, I see and hear nothing around me. I know there must be sirens and people coming out of their houses, but I see a white blur surrounding us as my world stops. Nothing is in focus, except her face. I know there are sirens because I called them, and I see a faint outline of boots sloshing in the pool of blood belonging to Ana as it drips in long rivulets to the ground off my arm.

Ana saved me. She is like taking a big breath after holding it as long as you could as a kid in the pool. She put me back together, and I want us to be together, I need us to be together. Because of her, I thought I would never break again. I need to be with her.

I was going to tell her this on our walk this morning, only now I'm not sure I'll ever get the chance. I love her, and even though she saved me, there is absolutely nothing I can do to save her right now.

I can't break my trance. I can't focus on anything but her face as our life together— what we were, what we are now, and what we could be— flashes before my eyes in black and white. Fast and slow all at once. As I see it flash before me, I can't make out what is true, and what is only a figment of my tangled imagination, my vision of a future we may never have.

Fall, Three Years Ago

"I fell in love with the girl at the rock show"
-Blink 182

Knox

"WHAT THE FUCK ARE you doing?"

My best friend Ethan breaks me out of my daze as we walk down a flight of stairs to the floor of a small concert, in a dive bar across town. The pungent smell of stale beer, sweat, and old wood fills the small space. Lights flash from the stage at the front of the room, and the band's music is almost deafening in the cramped room. We weave and push our way to the middle of the crowded pit right in front of the stage, and my heart beats in my chest in tandem with the base of the speakers thumping nearby.

It is the first week of October, just after our senior year of college. For the last five months, Ethan and I have finally been in the same place after the longest year of my life. Partying with my best friend should be all I want to do. Tonight though, all I want to do is get high as fuck, or bury myself in a bottle of whiskey or April, the blond I'd met at a party last month. She's a little much, but her tits bounce perfectly when I fuck her and her mouth looks great wrapped around my dick.

While the last few months have intensified my infatuation with getting my dick wet, Ethan, on the other hand, has found his new favorite pastime, going to random shows for up-and-coming rock bands who are making it "big" on Spotify. It's way less therapeutic if you ask me, but tonight, he invited me along. So far, not worth the $75 ticket.

I look at him, not really registering the question. I give absolutely no fucks about being here, and literally only came to distract myself from self-destruction at home in my bed alone.

"Why the hell did you say you would come with me tonight if you are just going to be a miserable dick all goddamn night?" His frustration is clear as he eyes me with annoyance.

I don't answer him, instead I focus on the pills I'm gliding between my fingers in my pocket, like smooth marbles. I have been clean for ten months. Those are words I would have never in my life pictured myself saying. I haven't told him the news yet, my injury is worse than they initially thought. I didn't want to put a damper on the night.

Great fucking job I'm doing at that.

After my elbow injury at baseball practice, I had surgery and was prescribed Oxy for pain management. The first pill was like a warm embrace, dulling the sharp edges of discomfort. By the second day, relief was more than physical; it was a comforting haze I found surprisingly fucking enjoyable. On the third day, the ache was almost gone, but goddam cravings had settled in. It was three days post-op, when the subtle shift took place, the twinge of excitement brought by the thought of the next dose. As each dose would start to wear off, panic would set in, a gnawing need for a comforting veil. The craving was swift and definite. I moved from sitting at the foot of my bed to pacing the room, over and over again, all while pressing my index and middle finger against my thumb in small circular motions. The small motion failed to be the distraction I was seeking as I was waiting for the nurse to bring me my next dose.

In hindsight, I should have known something was wrong, I should have said something then. Instead, I found myself requesting a refill of the prescription at my first post-op appointment, a request granted without question.

However, when I called to request it again only two weeks later, after they had given me a month's supply, the alarm bells rang. The doctor denied the request without an in person visit. During my appointment, the doctor examined my shoulder and we both agreed the pain I was experiencing was no longer being caused by my recent surgery. He began talking about the dangers of opioid misuse, and revelation struck me. I was abusing my pain meds, and if I didn't get my shit together and get help to turn things around quickly, I would be battling a full on opioid addiction.

I had stopped doing my exercises, skipped rehab appointments, and stopped hanging out with Ethan. Talking with the doctor, I admitted how I found myself having internal conversations, the most repetitive fucking conversations of my life. *Only a few more hours*, I'd tell myself. *Only 10 more minutes*. I would count the hours, minutes, and even seconds until my next fix. Each time the craving got more and more intense.

After the appointment he gave me a prescription to help with withdrawals, but they failed to be effective. I had severe withdrawal symptoms. One night, my mom walked into our house, her hands full of food bags. I was chewing the skin on the corner of my finger, pacing, wearing a path in the carpet. With raised brows and concern across her face, she didn't have to say a word. I blurted out the words on my own as I crashed into her arm like a small child in need of comfort from a storm. For me the storm was not outside, but raging inside me, with no escape for comfort.

Before I even knew it the words were leaving my mouth as I spoke with an urgency in my voice I didn't recognize, "Mom, I need more Oxy."

She took me straight to the hospital and from there I was admitted for medical monitoring.

After my hospital stay, it never really occurred to me the numb feeling would be something I'd crave again.

After the detox, I was so caught up in the idea of getting better. I did every small exercise I was given, ate right, and did any little bits of cardio I could each day. I'd go to parties at night, like a typical college student. I lieu of alcohol, I'd cap the night off between the legs of a hot chick, most recently, April. I was a focused student, and so optimistic about getting better and returning to the field. Oxy never seemed to cross my mind, and I thought I was over the hump.

But after finding out this motherfucking injury is career-ending, physical therapy isn't helping as much as it should be, and I might need a second surgery, I'm not feeling very optimistic.

This morning it occurred to me the only fucking thing I have to fall back on is a General Studies degree I only chose because I was positive I wouldn't need it. My future dissolved like sugar in the rain, and washed away like it never even fucking existed at all.

Now, my mental state is in fucking shambles, and I'm craving that numb feeling, that calm haze, where I feel nothing but want for another fix. A feeling I haven't been able to satiate.

I've been rolling two pills around like marbles in my pocket for the last few hours, debating getting them since Mom and I met with the doctor. Tonight, the craving is too much, so I got some pills from a guy known on campus. Not how I envisioned myself making a reappearance after graduation, but nothing feels right anymore. If a few shots at the bar don't scratch that itch, down the hatch these motherfuckers go!

The only thing that has kept me from taking them for the past two days is how slippery I know the slope is, and given my current state, I'm not sure I'll be strong enough to stop this time. This time I might fall too deep into a numb abyss, not having the future I expected motivating me to pull myself out. So instead, I roll them around debating giving into the craving or continuing to act like a prick to my best friend, holding my disappointment close.

It's not his fault, and he's going to have my ass when he finds out I haven't told him. He didn't even know I had the fucking appointment, he thinks it's in two weeks. I didn't want to have to talk about it if this was the outcome. So I lied and now I'm acting like a giant piece of shit.

"Sorry man, let's hit the bar! I need a drink!" I yell over the music.

"What's your deal? You're not supposed to be drinking," Ethan says.

"Nothing, ok? I'm fine!" I shout, my voice strained.

"Listen, I can't be your babysitter." Ethan huffs and heads toward the bar, leaving me to follow with a sinking feeling in my chest. I walk behind him, shooting a text to April.

Her response comes through before I can put my phone away.

Me: Wanna come over tonight?

April: Can't tonight. I'm at my parents.

Disappointed, I have my head down, shifting my focus back to the smooth pills still rolling slowly between my index finger and thumb. If I can't bury myself in April, whiskey will have to do! With each step I take in the dimly lit bar, the weight of my torture helps my debate set in. Will whiskey's burning solace win or the numb escape of pills? My mind is a battlefield with each thought crashing together as I take my hand out of my pocket to pull out my wallet, hoping deep down whiskey will win and I won't have to resort to the pills.

Just as I look up to give the bartender my order, my heart stops in my chest. Time seems to have come to a standstill, and the world around me blurs into a soft fog. I am now numb to the pain just in my chest, the turmoil, the internal battle. It all fucking melted away. Just like that, it's gone like the little puffs of smoke disappearing off the joints filling the room around us.

I am frozen, face to face with pure beauty that's un-matched. She's not just some hot chick who grabs your attention, she's more than that. As I stare at her, I realize her beauty might not be obvious to everyone. It's quiet and reserved, but for me, it is strong, yelling out above the noise on stage. She wears little makeup, just something on her lashes, and a slight sheen to her lips. Her skin is a tapestry of tiny beauty marks, each of them creating the character sometimes missing with the presence of too much makeup. Small beads of sweat curl the fallen hairs from her dark brown messy bun, causing my attention to trace each curl to the very top of the strands. But her eyes, fuck, they light up her face, enveloped by the tiniest dark circles somehow enhancing their bright blue hues instead of making her look tired like most people. Her smile though, that's the main attraction. It makes me want to stare at her all night, with her slightly cherry lips while not particularly full, are pure fucking perfection.

I wonder what they would look like, slightly swollen and stretched from my cock?

I want to memorize every detail. Her features are not what I am usually drawn to, and she is completely sucking me in. I can't look away. "What can I get you?" she asks.

You.

"I'll have a Coke." Suddenly, I'm feeling numb to everything except her and wanting to make damn sure I remember every second.

"And a beer," Ethan says behind me.

Shit, I forgot he is here.

"I got it, man."

"Thanks. Hey, the next few songs on their set list are what made me want to come see this band live, so I'm gonna head back while you pay." He grabs the beer as soon as she sets it down, but before he heads back to the pit in front of the stage he pauses, "Not sure what the sudden shift was, but I'm glad you passed on the alcohol."

I tip my soda in his direction acknowledging his words of encouragement and then refocus my attention, watching her every move as she runs my card. I watch her chew on the corner of her lip as she swipes the card, her fingers dancing lazily over the buttons. My eyes trace the path of a small bead of sweat from her hairline down her forehead, ending at the top of her eyebrow. This chick is more than meets the eye, I just know it."Here you go." She hands me my card and gives me a fucking smile with her tongue darting out to lick her lips.

"Appreciate it," I say, walking away.

Drink in hand, I make my way back down to the floor. Ethan is lost in the music and I am lost in the sight behind the bar. I keep looking back over my shoulder to try and get a peek at her, but there are too many people. After nursing my soda for three songs, distracted by thoughts of her, I "drop" it on the floor, looking for an excuse to slide back up to the bar. The contents splash Ethan's shoes.

"Are you kidding me, man?" Ethan asks with a roll of his eyes.

"Shit, sorry!" Picking up the half-empty can I add, "I'll be back." Then I head back to the bar for a new drink.

This time, instead of sliding my fingers across the pills in my pocket, I'm clenching and unclenching my fists as my stomach flips and turns with nerves. I've never been this damn nervous about talking with some random chick. Quite the opposite, actually. I'm kind of a cocky sonofabitch. I'm trying to channel my usual overconfidence to dull the nerves as I approach the bar, but it's nowhere to be found. As a star athlete in college, the conversation never really mattered. Chicks were eager for my company the second I looked in their direction. So this pit in my stomach making it feel like my insides are dancing with the base on the drums, is new to me. I take a deep breath and bite my very new lip ring, feeling a slight sting of pain as she asks, "Back again?"

Fuck me…

"Yup, some asshole spilled my Coke."

"I'll grab you another one. Water? Anything else?" she asks as she bends down, reaching into the cooler in front of her.

Fucking, you.

"Your number," I say with a smug ass grin.

"Nice try," she chuckles. "Your cheeky smile might usually work, but not on me, you're wasting your time."

"Not interested?" I challenge, my grin widening despite the sting of rejection.

"Nope!" she says, popping the "p".

This chick. Bet.

"Guess I'll just have to change your mind," I say with my most charming smile.

She stares, expressionless, "Five dollars."

"Five dollars for a Coke is outright theft," I say.

"Maybe you shouldn't have spilled it," she responds clearly onto me.

Ok. I'll bite.

Without saying a word, eyes never leaving her, I tap my card on the reader and then walk away, not looking back. As I make my way back to Ethan, plotting my next move, I am pleasantly surprised when he stops me halfway.

"Going to get a beer, be back in sec," he says.

Fucking perfect.

"I'll go get you one. I owe you for being such a dick tonight."

"Thanks, man," he says and turns, heading back to the show.

As I move my ass closer to the bar, swagger in every step, she makes eye contact with me and rolls her bright blue eyes. I stand at the back of the now-long line and stare. She tries to avoid making eye contact with me, only allowing herself to glance for one second. Each time, her smile gets slightly more pronounced. When I finally reach the front, she hands me a Coke without saying a word.

"Five dollars."

"You don't even know what I want," I say sarcastically.

"Fine, what can I get you?" she asks with a smart-ass smile on her face.

"A beer." I try to mirror her expression.

She doesn't even flinch, no smile, no eye roll. "Twelve dollars."

I tap my card with a smile, looking her over as I slide it back in my wallet, and then back away slowly, taking my time, making sure my confidence is clear. I take a slow sip of my drink with a grin, enjoying the cool crisp liquid as it slides down my throat. I have never worked this hard to get a girl's number before, especially not for someone so fucking adamant to turn me down. Usually by this point I've lost interest and refocused my attention. What is it about her?

"This band is killing it," Ethan shouts over the music, interrupting my thoughts.

"Yeah," I say, looking in the direction of the bar.

Ethan enjoys the next several songs, and I nod to the music as I sip my drink. After another 3 or 4 songs, both of our drinks are empty, and my neck is sore from the strain of trying to steal glances of her over the crowd. "I'm going to get us another round," I tell Ethan. On the short walk over to the bar, I try to think of a way to break her cool exterior. I get to the top of the ramp near the bar, only to make eye contact with a tall redhead behind the bar, not my beautiful brunette. My stomach sinks.

Damn.

Looking around for a few minutes while I wait in line, I realize she is nowhere to be found. When I get to the front of the line, I order our drinks. I scan the bar several times while I wait for the girl who is a few inches too tall to bring me our drinks. Disappointed, I tap my card to pay and I make my way back down the ramp to the crowded pit where Ethan is bouncing his head to the music. I keep scanning the room, searching for her everywhere, but spotting a short brunette in a dark room with flashing lights proves harder than I thought. Every time I scan I come up empty.

The rest of the show drags on agonizingly slow, the sounds of the music blurring into irrelevant murmurs. Sounds invading my mind, distracting me from my thoughts. When it finally ends, I can't wait to get the fuck out of here, kicking myself for missing my shot. Ethan and I push through the crowd, heading for the door.

Stepping outside, I feel relief taking over as the cool air hits my heated skin. I close my eyes and take a deep breath, allowing the cold air to invade my lungs.

It was hotter than a stripper's tit, in there.

My phone pings with a message and I pull it out to see who is texting when I step on Ethan's shoe and twist my ankle.

"Fuck, man!" I grumble as I slide my phone back into my pocket, trying to steady myself. Then I realize it's not Ethan's shoe I stepped on.

"You are relentless, you know that?"

No fucking way.

I smile looking up from where I put my phone only to be face to face with her.

As the smile spreads across my face... she fucking smiles back.

"Ana," she says as she reaches out her hand.

It's one word, her name. Simple and breathtaking just like her. I never knew a name could fit someone so goddam perfectly.

"Knox," I say with a smile, placing my hand in hers for the handshake she initiated. When our hands meet, my entire body tingles in response.

"Hmm, that's not what I was expecting," She chuckles.

"What were you expecting?" I ask, dropping my smile, confused, my ego a little bruised.

"I don't know, something a little more generic, maybe a little more fuckboyish like Chad or Brad," she says with a shrug.

"I don't even know what the fuck to say to that," I laugh.

My phone pings for the second time but I can't bring myself to break my gaze as we stand staring at each other. I am lost in her eyes, which stare back at me expression-less. She is a real ballbuster, and I can't help but want her to *fucking* crush mine to pieces.

"What the fuck, man! I've been texting you for five minutes. I have to work tomorrow," an annoyed voice bellows from across the street.

Ethan, shit!

I forgot he was here, again, or better yet didn't realize he wasn't here as he yelled across the crowd breaking my gaze. We must have gotten separated and I didn't notice. I look back at Ana, knowing time is not on my side, patience is not Ethan's thing.

"Dude, fuck off for a second," I yell across the crowded sidewalk.

Turning to Ana I ask, "Did I change your mind?"

"What?" Confusion crosses her face.

"Well, I asked for your number earlier, and you're still here… so…" I let the words die out as I tuck my hands in my pockets.

"No," she says flatly for the second time tonight.

Her gaze holds mine for a long second and then she turns to walk away. My stomach is in fucking knots as I panic, trying desperately to find the words lost on my tongue, wanting her to stop, to turn around, anything. But I just stand here with my hands in my pockets, not a fucking word leaving my mouth.

I have no game with this chick.

"Knox!" I turn towards Ethan who is yelling my name again with a smug ass grin on his face, that makes me want to smack it right off. His look, mirroring the prick I've been towards him all night.

Fucking cock block.

I start to walk away. He knows exactly what he is doing, getting me back by making me leave before I can chase after her to get her number. Fucker probably doesn't even have to work tomorrow. My phone buzzes again and just as I open it to read the text from April just came through, a hand brushes my arm. It is so soft I almost miss it.

"Knox," Ana says softly.

I quickly shove my phone back into my pocket.

"I'll be at that diner tomorrow morning at 9am," she says pointing at the old building across the parking lot. It has a neon sign flashing "The Pit" and looks like the lights are about to go out. I look in the direction she is pointing, and when I look back, she's gone.

"I'm going to fucking kick your ass in the morning. I have to work at 7, you asshole!" Ethan says as I saunter up next to him with a sly grin on my face, my hands buried in my pockets again. *I guess this asshole does have work. Humm.* "Leave it to you to line up some ass at a random concert," he laughs as we climb into the car.

I start gliding those smooth little pills between my index finger and thumb again and continue for the entire ride back to Ethan's apartment. I didn't bother answering him, there was no point. For now, I'll let him believe what he wants. I turn up the music and we joke and talk shit back and forth the entire ride home, and I forget all about how my life went up in smoke and just let myself be.

It takes us about 25 minutes to get back to Ethan's, we fist-bump and I get in my Jeep, headed home. It's a short drive, only a few blocks over to my parents' house, but it's consumed with flashes of Ana's perfectly imperfect face. Her bright blue eyes, and fuck me, that smile! I can't wait for 9 am tomorrow.

I walk into my room, pull my phone out of my pocket with one hand, and pull my shirt over my head with the other. I slide my pants off, the motion making those little pills go tumbling across the floor. I stare at them for just one second, bend down, pick them up, and make my way to the nightstand, putting them back in the little pill container inside. I have a new craving taking over. The new addiction feels good. All I want is one more smile from Ana. Being in her presence numbed my pain for those few minutes. Just what I've been looking for. I'm exhausted as I fall into bed. I roll over, set my alarm, and smile as sleep pulls me under.

This was the very first loop of the thread she'd weave that would eventually put me back together.

Ana

MY ALARM WAS SET for 7:00 am, but right now it's 6:52 and I've already been awake for 15 minutes. I don't know who I thought I was kidding thinking I'd get any sleep. I'm pacing around my room frantically, changing my outfit for the 3rd time in the last 10 minutes. I showered when I got home from work, trying to wash the smell of smoke, alcohol, and sweat off my body and out of my hair. I love bartending, but when the club holds concerts, I hate my life. There is just a different energy, one sending up a smoke signal saying, "Spill EVERY damn drink on the bartender!"

Now, I can't seem to find clothes that feel right. What do you wear at 9 am when you are going to meet the hottest guy you have ever laid eyes on who you were purposely an ass to all night and now you're not quite sure you even want to go?

I'm usually quiet and reserved, with a no-bullshit kind of energy. I can't stand fake people. I can't stand guys who think they are a gift to any woman lucky enough to be graced by their presence, and that's the big dick energy Knox was giving off.

I will do anything for anyone I love, but easy to get… that's not me! I make guys work hard to be in my presence, hell I even make my friends prove themselves before I open up. That's probably why my circle is so small, I don't even know you could call it a circle, but I don't care, it's something I take great pride in. It's me and Blake, that's it, more like two points on the ends of a very short line. I guess I would also include my brother, Ryan, making it more of a triangle of support. He and Blake are my best support system when shit goes sideways.

I had no intention of going out with Knox, his cocky demeanor is not for me. His blond hair and emerald eyes though… those are definitely for me, and his lip ring, SHIT! Facial piercings don't usually do it for me, but on him, fuck, it's hot.

He was a little too sure of himself though, too persistent, and I couldn't stand it, so I texted my best friend, Blake, also my favorite coworker, to switch bars with me during the concert. I moved to the rooftop bar and forgot Knox existed for the rest of the night. Sure he's hot, but I've watched Blake crash and burn with too many guys just like Knox, and have learned to steer clear of them.

When he bumped into me outside, and I could tell he had no idea it was me, he looked so genuine. One of the most genuine smiles I have ever seen. I felt like maybe the universe had different plans, and was screaming a secret message to me over the sound of the crowd. I watched his smile take over his face and it made me second-guess what I had assumed about him. So I decided to make him sweat it out a little bit and then made an arrogant-ass move myself. I walked away, let him watch me, and then turned back around and told him where he could find me the next day, the insinuation of an invitation lingering in the air.

Not something I would *ever* typically do.

One tiny out of character action kept me up all night tossing and turning, and ended with me waking before my alarm, something I also *never* do; anyone who knows me knows just how much I love my sleep and sleeping in.

With my mind a high-speed train of thoughts zipping by faster than I can register them, I stop and take a look at myself in the mirror. I decide on my black-worn jeans and light pink tank, and finish off the outfit with my black leather jacket and combat boots. I bend down to tie one of my boots as Blake sits on the end of my bed.

"Leaving it all to the imagination with that one aren't you?" she asks.

"He's lucky I even changed my mind, Blake," I say as I smooth my hands down the front of the tank. "I'm not trying to impress anyone. I like to be comfortable."

"That's what I love about you the most!" she says. "You give absolutely zero fucks."

"Plus," I continue, "he looks like he's used to girls who get all dolled up with their tits out just for him, and that's not me. I want to be *very* clear about who I am."

"I'm not sure anyone could possibly confuse who you are, Ana. You are blunt as fuck. There isn't a soul out there more true to themselves than you are. Are you nervous he won't show?"

"No!" I say a little too quickly tossing my hair in a ponytail. "He'll show, he's too presumptuous not to."

"Then why is there a pile of clothes on your floor with a path practically worn in the carpet from your closet to the mirror?" she jokes.

"*He* makes me nervous, I'm not sure I even want to go anymore," I say as I apply my mascara and lip balm.

"What? Nervous how? No one makes you nervous. You read people better than anyone I know. Maybe you shouldn't go, Ana," Blake says with concern etched on her face.

"Not like that! Not in a creepy way, or an intimidating way. He's just so hot, Blake," I drag out the word hot for emphasis. "and usually, *hot* doesn't matter to me. When he gave me his little smirk last night with a slight eyebrow raise and played with that damn lip ring, I got all jittery and couldn't think straight. I turned on my bitch face because it was my only armor. But he broke through it, Blake! I NEVER do shit like that! I never *play* hard to get, I'm usually just hard to fucking get. I'm always so true to myself, so collected." I look her right in the eyes, feeling like my heart is beating a thousand miles a minute. "That's what makes me so nervous. It freaks me out. I had one damn interaction with Knox, and I'm not myself."

"You like him…" she says with an eyebrow wiggle.

"I don't even know him," I tell her as I grab my purse.

"Maybe you want to," she smiles as she walks out of my room and a few seconds later I hear the soft click of the bathroom door.

I don't even know him.

It's 8:45 am. I decided to come early to get some coffee in my system before facing Knox this morning. I'm not a morning person, so every second I have to fully wake up will be a gift for Knox. As I walk into The Pit I'm instantly drawn to Knox sitting at the counter with a cup of coffee. I didn't even have to let my eyes wander around to find him. They are drawn to him like a magnet, moving in his direction on their own accord, faster than my brain can signal them to do so. Standing here taking him in, my breath hitches. His slightly long dirty blond hair is tucked beneath a hat curling around the edges in the back. He is in a black hoodie and jeans. I swear, if I had walked in here and his hoodie would have been over his hat, I might have melted. There is just something about that look, it gets me every damn time. I can't see his eyes as he thumbs through his phone, but I just know the black hoodie and hat will make them an even more vibrant green.

"Have you been here long?" I ask as I pull out the stool next to him.

"Just a bit," he says with a soft smile. "Do you want to get a table?"

"No, this is great! I prefer to sit here. Better people watching," I say with a laugh.

"I fucking love people-watching," he responds.

"Listen, Knox," I say, taking a long breath and turning to face him. I decided on the way here that even though I was not myself last night, I would be nothing but myself this morning. "I am going to be honest with you because that's who I am, I'm a straight shooter. I don't like bullshit. I'm not interested in the flippant playboy attitude you had last night. I know most girls love that shit, and probably eat it up, but I'm not one of them. I only spend my time with people who earn my time. I don't play around. For some reason, one I can't quite put my finger on, I like you enough to invite you to sit here with me while I have a cup of coffee and a cinnamon roll. I don't know why, because last night you drove me nuts. I even switched bars to avoid you. But I'm here because I want to be, so can we just hang out and skip all of the bullshit?"

His smile widens as he looks past me and as I turn the waitress sets down two cinnamon rolls.

"Well this is a little *too* perfect if you ask me," he chuckles. "I saw 'Best Cinnamon Rolls in Town' on the menu, so it felt like it was a safe option," he says with a chuckle. "Can we get another cup of coffee?" Knox asks the waitress when she returns with two forks.

"No bullshit huh?" He pauses for a second. "Well, that little rant of yours was hot as hell, Ana. A girl who knows what she wants is such a turn on. I don't exactly know what the fuck to say to that, but I know I'm a cocky motherfucker, so I can't make any promises. But I will try…" The words fade out like he doesn't know the right ones and then he just smiles and rolls his lip ring between his teeth, and my stomach lurches at the small action.

We spent the next hour and a half talking and laughing, creating our own stories for people in the restaurant as we drank our coffee.

"That guy," Knox whispers pointing to a man sitting alone in a booth across from us, phone in hand scrolling extremely fast through whatever he is looking at, "His suit and tie must be really fucking tight, I think the oxygen is cut off to his balls, making him panic, and it's coming out in his urgent as fuck scrolling. How is he even seeing anything on his phone?"

I pick up my mug and take a sip of coffee as I move my eyes in the direction he is pointing and the second I catch a glimpse of what he is talking about, I spit my coffee out all over Knox with a laugh.

"Shit, sorry!" I say as I reach over and urgently start wiping his face. He just laughs and takes the napkin from my hand and continues to clean himself up. His laugh is deep and slightly metallic, sending a warmth through me I wasn't prepared for.

"So what do you do when you're not bartending?" he asks.

"Hang out at home… read… I love being cuddled up in a blanket with a book. That's something my roommate and I have in common," I explain.

"What about you?" I ask.

"I just moved back after graduation, so I'm still trying to find my footing and figure out what's next. Right now most of my time is spent hanging out with my friend Ethan, the one you saw last night," he says.

"Ah, the one who was pissed at you last night for keeping him out too late… I remember," I say with a smirk looking curiously over my shoulder. "Why do so many couples sit on the same side of the booth? It would make me so uncomfortable."

He laughs, "Why?"

"Several reasons. One, you have to turn to talk. Two, the other side of the table is empty. Three," I look him straight in the eyes, so that he knows how serious I am about this in case he's lucky enough to get a second date, "If your not talking to each other your just making un-comfortable eye contact with the rest of the restaurant."

"Yeah, but no one can see your hands under the table." He shifts in his seat as if he thinks his comment was too much. "Are pancakes your favorite breakfast food?" he asks changing the subject. Yep, he thinks he went to far.

I give him a comforting smile, "No, I'm a sucker for cinnamon rolls, and coffee, I wonder what people would say about us while people-watching."

"That I'm outkicking my coverage."

"I've never heard that before," I know I look puzzled.

"They probably would think you're way out of my league," he responds without hesitation. "But, that's a good thing. They'll wonder how I got you and assume it's because I have something to offer that they can't see, if you know what I mean," He says, wiggling his brows.

I laugh, "Wow… your cockiness really has no bounds."

He smiles as he sips his coffee and the green in his eyes sparkles as the light reflects off them.

"Call me cocky all you want. I like hearing the word cock come out of that sweet mouth of yours." He winks and I immediately feel a blush burning my cheeks.

After I recovered and we agreed to cut the bullshit, it turned out to be one of the most natural conversations I'd ever had with someone I'd just met. It felt like we'd been friends and known each other for years.

Knox Reed is actually pretty funny. He is also an asshole, just like he owned up to, but I kind of like it. There is something so sexy about a person who is unapologetically themself.

Last night I suggested The Pit as a meeting place because I had to be at the bar at 11:00 am for a mandatory staff meeting. When I looked down and saw 10:30 on my phone, I found myself disappointed that the time had gone by so fast, which was surprising considering I almost didn't come at all. I wanted to be close to work so I could claim my meeting was earlier if this turned out to be a bust, but right now I wish I didn't actually have a meeting to go to.

"I really don't want to cut this short, but I have a meeting at the bar in about 30 minutes," I say with a disappointed sigh.

"Well, I'm glad you feel like this was too short too," he says, twisting his coffee mug in his hands. Then he looks up, eyes piercing me, "Ana," he pauses. "Can I have your number? I'd like to do this again, maybe when we have more time," He seems so shy all of a sudden.

Maybe I did read him wrong.

I have no self control, because I also want to do this again when we have more time. I put my hand out, and he places his phone in my palm with a grin spreading across his face. I type in my number and create a new contact and save my name and number. I definitely read him wrong. Besides Blake, I have never had so much fun just talking to someone. After we finished our coffee, he paid the bill and offered to walk me across the parking lot, which I agreed to.

Just as we stepped out of The Pit's front doors, Knox cleared his throat, "Would it be cool if I hold your hand?"

I was putty in his hands. My stomach turned in knots, my heart sped up when I put my hand out, his rough calloused fingers slowly intertwined with mine. I lost my breath. The quick walk across the parking lot went by in slow motion, and I memorized every twitch of his fingers, the feeling of his thumb as it caressed the palm of my hand in slow circles. The way he kept hold of my hand as I pulled my backpack out of the back of my car and then he took it from me and slung it over his shoulder so he could carry it for me. When we reached the bar door, we said a quick goodbye, then stepped into each other with a hug- deep and comforting. He laid a small kiss on my forehead. Our goodbye was simple, no bullshit, but it had me feeling all warm inside.

As I walked inside the bar I was replaying our conversation and realizing how quickly I opened up to him. Sharing simple things about myself I usually kept close to my chest until I knew people better.

I even told him about my dad. When I was in high school, my dad had an affair with a coworker. My mom went to surprise him with lunch, and walked in on him balls deep, mid-thrust. It was all very cliche, but it ruined my otherwise picture perfect family. My relationship with my dad has never been the same, and I have become very skeptical of any man who exudes any type of player persona. The last thing I want is to think I have found the love of my life, only to be devastated by the harsh reality he's incapable of loving one woman. I saw what it did to my mom, and I can't bring myself to forgive him completely.

Sharing this detail of my life with Knox, lifted a weight off my shoulders I didn't know I carried. There is something freeing about letting go of my inhibitions and doing something I would never do. Living life in calculated motions, always in control, and never truly taking risks, is comfortable and soothing, like a warm bath on a cool day. However, Knox brings out a side of me I have never tapped into, never been in touch with.

Knox Reed is going to be the death of me, I don't know who I am when I'm with him, but I kind of like her.

Buzzz. I lift my phone to look at the new message.

Knox: Talk to you later.

Me: Maybe…

Today, March 1

"Have you loved like this before?"
-Blink 182

Ana

"**A**NA, NO, NO, NO, come on baby just open your eyes."

This is the first thing I hear, this is actually the only thing I hear over the sirens in the distance. This has been the soundtrack on repeat for a long time now. Quiet, muting the background, interrupting my dreams. His voice is pulling me back, but now with my eyes closed, unable to move, reality hits me. All I see in the darkness are memories, the first time I saw his face, the first time I kissed him. *He* is mine.

I don't want him to see me.

Not like this.

Not right now.

I just feel pain, and I'm not sure where it's coming from or how bad it actually hurts.

I hear Knox, and I feel his hand frantically running through my hair as he peppers my face with little kisses, but I can't open my eyes, and I can't stay awake. It hurts too bad.

I hear footsteps, and as they grow louder I can't focus.

Is he here?

Take him away! Take him away! Take him away!

He can't see me like this!

Knox keeps stealing my thoughts. He keeps replaying little broken bits of time spent together, I need him to stop for just a second, just for one damn second so I can hear what is happening beyond us. So I can hear what I can't see. But I can't, he keeps stealing my thoughts. It's soft, quiet, I'm not even sure he knows he is saying it out loud, but as I fall back into darkness I continue to relive the stories Knox is telling me in broken bits. I listen to his memories as he whispers them and I remember mine.

Knox, please, please, shut the fuck up for one second, please, plea…

But, he doesn't and as I listen to his voice it pulls me back to sleep. The bright hazel eyes, chestnut hair, and tan skin consuming my mind are overtaken by visions of a tall man with dirty blond hair and the brightest emerald eyes I have ever seen.

Knox's words take over, and fill my mind as I replay them like a live action movie in my dreams, small splintered pieces that have built our current reality.

Fall, Three Years Ago

"Let's go, don't wait, this night's almost over"
-Blink 182

Knox

A NA MENTIONED HER MEETING was only an hour, and she has dinner plans with her roommate at 8:00 tonight. So, I have one hour to plan. I cross my fingers she'll agree to spend the next 8 hours with me.

It takes me the entire hour to plan out our day. I start by moving my Jeep to the very front of the parking lot outside the door she went in, so there's no way she can miss me.

When it comes to romance, I have no idea what I'm doing, but she makes me want to give it a solid try. It's not even sex that's driving me, I mean it would be fucking amazing, to have her lips on any part of me. If her smile is this fucking good, I can't help but imagine her face and those lips as she moans my name. The real thing driving me is her goddamn smile. It does something to me, makes me want to spend as much time with her as I possibly can.

Just as I finish purchasing tickets for the maple festival, hoping I don't waste them, I hear the door to the bar swing open. About 10 people come walking out laughing when I see a flash of red behind the small group. Next to the tall redhead is Ana rummaging through her purse. She quickly slips something across her lips and tucks it back in her purse just as the text message I send hits her phone. She pulls it out and slowly makes eye contact with me from outside the door.

> **Me:** Look up

> **Ana:** …

The small bubbles on the phone flash a few times as she holds her phone in her hand while looking right at me. She looks at the redhead next to her, I see her lips moving but can't hear what they are saying. Ana hands her the backpack we had grabbed from her car after breakfast, and slowly walks my way. I hop out of my Jeep and meet her at the passenger door.

"What are you still doing here?" she chuckles, tucking a fallen hair from her ponytail behind her ear.

"Spend the day with me?" I ask, trying not to sound too desperate.

Ana takes a deep breath, like she is trying to think better of it and find a way to turn me down. I watch as she pulls out her phone, snaps a picture of me and shoots off a text, and says, "I have to be back here by 6 so I'm not late to dinner with my roommate, Blake."

"What is the picture for?" I awkwardly chuckle, readjusting my hat.

"I sent it to my brother and Blake, you know, in case you murder me, chop my body into a million tiny pieces and bury them in a shallow grave in a random river somewhere," she responds seriously. "Wave… and smile, she's staring at you, and if you don't look friendly, she'll insist on coming along."

"True crime Podcast junkie?" I ask as I wave and smile trying to silently reassure her roommate she's in good hands. Then I lean past Ana opening the car door for her.

"Yes," she responds proudly as she climbs in.

"Deal," I respond, relieved I'd get to spend a little more time looking at her fucking smile. "I'll have you back by 6, and I won't murder you and chop you up into tiny pieces."

Fall in Vermont is in full swing, the air is cool and crisp, and the trees in October are unmatched. As we start our short 10 mile drive down a two-lane highway lined on both sides with trees covered in vibrant red and orange leaves, I reach over the console to hold her hand, and to my surprise, she settles in the seat leaning slightly in my direction and pulls one foot up on the seat reaching her arm across her shin. I could get used to this. She's been prying since we started our drive for me to tell her where we are going, but I wouldn't. As we approach our destination, I see a faint smile peek through on those beautiful cherry lips of hers. She sits up to get a better look over the dash, "Knox, are we going to the maple festival?" Without allowing time for a response she continues, "I love the maple festival, I used to go with my Grandpa Scott every year when he was still alive."

"Yeah? What's your favorite part?" I ask.

She sits up even straighter in the seat staring right at the side of my face as I drive into the parking lot. "Walking through the apple orchard in the back. Everyone is so busy moving from each table testing maple samples, getting maple apple cider, riding the hayride, and playing the lawn games that the orchard is quiet. A little haven right there, under everyone's nose."

"Sounds pretty cool," I say.

Anything would be good coming out of her mouth. Her eyes get big and she can't sit still as she talks about the festival and all the things she and her grandpa used to do. I chuckle as I pull the tickets up on my email and send her ticket to her phone as I listen to her.

"My Grandpa and I would stay until closing time," she continues, "and after the movie on the lawn, my grandpa would always sweet talk one of the employees out of a few leftover treats to eat on the drive home. The maple caramels are my absolute favorite!" she says with the biggest smile I have ever seen. "Knox, I can't wait! I can't believe this is where we're going!" She sits up a little taller in her seat and turns to me, "You really are a cocky sonofabitch, Knox."

"What?" I ask with a laugh.

"You were so sure I would agree to go with you that you bought these tickets before you even talked to me about it."

"I was not sure at all. But you are a gamble worth taking," I smile. "Do you want to stay a little longer than I originally planned?" I ask, hoping she will say yes. "I was planning on having you back by 6:00, but I can make sure to have you back by 6:45, so we could have a little more time," I wait for her response as she plays with the zipper on her jacket, clearly deep in thought.

"You know what, I can just go to dinner like this. As long as I'm back in my car by 7:45 I'll be good. I'm meeting Blake at a place right by the bar. Plus the festival closes at 7:30, and I would love to see the movie on the lawn," she smiles.

The things I would do for that smile.

As we walk into the festival the smell of maple fills the air. For most people, the smell can be a little much, but to me, it feels like home. "Right there is my favorite memory of this festival from when I was younger," I say pointing to the baseball fields outside the gate. "When I was in Little League we would play the same fall tournament every year, and after the games, the team would come here together. All of the parents would stand around drinking spiked cider and beer, play the lawn games, and visit while we ran around. We would eat crap food all night, and go home smelling like maple and sweat. It was the happiest time for me as a kid."

"Do you still play?"

I stare at the ground debating on what to say, and how much to give, and then I decide to give her as much as I can. She wouldn't want half truths. She doesn't seem like someone who would appreciate pussy footing around a topic. I exhale once, gathering courage to tell the whole story.

"I just graduated in May. I was the starting pitcher for my college team going into our last season. I had scouts from the minors contacting my coach to set up times to check me out during the season. One night at indoor practice right before winter break, I was warming up in the cages with a buddy. Coach was sitting on a bucket giving us pointers, I stretched out both arms to throw a warm-up pitch, and right before I released the ball, I heard a pop and fell to the ground in excruciating pain. My elbow immediately started swelling and bruising. Coach rushed me to the trainer and she took me to the ER right off campus," I paused for a bit of courage to continue.

"About a week later at my follow-up, they decided I needed reconstructive surgery. I did everything they said after my surgery. I worked hard in PT, rested it, and iced it, but after about 16 weeks of therapy, my range of motion was not where it needed to be and I was still experiencing intermittent numbness." I have never told this story out loud. Everyone I know was experiencing it with me, so again I pause to take a long breath.

"They said it would all get better over time, but by that point, the season was underway, and the pitcher who replaced me was having a great season. I sat on the bench through the summer, optimistic I could still do spring tryouts for the minors, but a few days ago, my mom and I met with the surgeon for my final clearance. While my range of motion and numbness have improved, they are still not ideal, and the doctor is talking about another surgery to fix the ulnar nerve, but the outcome seems pretty bleak. The chances of a full recovery after a second surgery is very slim. It's likely that afterwards I will have to stop pitching and take on a different position. Even though I've been playing my whole life, I can't just start playing a new position and make it to the minors you know? College is over, and my baseball career is too. I could pick up games in some leagues in town, but it feels too futile. I wasn't even in a game when it happened, I went out on a fucking warm-up pitch at practice, I wasn't even pitching at full strength." I know she hears the shaking in my voice. Reliving this hell is too much, yet when I look at her face, all the turmoil raging inside me disappears. I don't really even know her, but she makes me want to feel again. The story is hard, but telling it to her feels comforting.

"I'm so sorry! I don't… I'm sorry," she repeats. "How are you doing with all that, it's a lot, Knox?" she finally asks.

"I'm in therapy, so that helps." I reflect on how far I've come. As time has passed, I've learned therapy isn't something I need to be shy about. It's honestly something I think everyone could benefit from. "It has pushed me to look at my injury as a loss, and space to grieve the career I thought I would be heading into right now."

We stood in silence for a few minutes just watching the people scurry around us.

I can't tell her about my addiction. Not yet, I can't scare her away.

"I wonder if we were ever here at the same time," Ana says softly as she looks over the crowd. With just those few words, my mind shifts from my shattered future to wondering if her words are true.

We spent the next three hours walking around the festival living our best lives and reliving our childhood memories together. We got caramel apples and hot chocolate while we walked around the different booths. We ate maple caramels and watched the street performers scattering entertainment across the grounds. We ate corn dogs from my favorite stand and played yard games, bags, giant Jenga, and lawn chess.

Tonight the movie on the lawn was one of my all-time favorite movies: Nightmare Before Christmas. There is something about Christmas and Halloween merging that just made cinematic history for me as a kid. There was about an hour and a half until the movie would start, so we walked over to a small cart and bought an overpriced blanket and snacks for the movie. Then we decided to kill time doing Ana's favorite thing at the festival, wandering around the apple orchard in the back.

"How is it so empty back here? I didn't even know this was here," I wonder out loud.

"The orchard is closed for picking during the festival days," she answers. "My Grandpa was friends with one of the landowners. He said they set up all of the events of the festival way up front away from the orchard and closed the stand where you get baskets and bags for picking. I guess the first year the festival was open they had apple picking as a part of the festivities and people would let their kids run back here and there were so many smashed and half-eaten apples, it was such a huge mess by the end of the three days so they decided they would lose too much money if they kept it open every year. It's not off-limits, but they don't advertise it's back here, which is why most people don't even know it's here."

"People suck," I reply.

Ana giggles and leads me through the wooden gate into the orchard. It's about 3:30 and by this point in the day, the sun is lower in the sky, cascading off the apple trees. She continues leading me to the back corner where there's a tall tree stump next to an old bench where I can see people have carved their names. It is a scene right out of a movie. A metal rod is tied to the tree and is just sharp enough to carve into the bark. She picks it up, "Let's add your name to the tree," she says looking for a good spot.

"Just mine? What about yours?" I ask, setting our blankets and snacks down next to the stump.

"My grandpa added mine the first time we came out here when I was about ten. I had to wait until I was ten to come with him so I was old enough to last the whole day," she explains as she searches the tree for her name. "Right there," she says with a sad smile as she points to the bottom. *Anabelle,* it says in choppy carved letters. *...Anabelle Scott.* I thought to myself, *How does a name get more fucking perfect?*

I watch Ana carve my name into the bark on the other side of the tree. As I watch her all I want to do is kiss her. Well, what I really want to do is touch her. Between her fingers being laced in mine all day, and the smell of her flowery shampoo hitting my nose when she moves past me, I find myself having to readjust my cock that's trying to bust through my jeans in hopes she doesn't take notice of what's going on down there.

I look up and am met with bright blue eyes and a stare much different than the one I got at the bar. I stare back and slowly reach out to tuck the loose hair falling from her ponytail behind her ear. Her breath shudders at the touch and she closes her eyes and lets out the smallest moan.

Fuck me.

I would have missed it if there had been any noise other than the soft wind in the trees. My cock stirs as I slowly bend down and brush a kiss on her forehead, my hand locked in place curled around the nape of her neck where I'd tucked the hair.

She smiles but backs away. I inhale slowly trying to steady my racing heart as I watch her walk over and pick two apples off the tree nearby. As she turns back in my direction, she offers me one and slowly lifts hers to her mouth. Her lips part and softly brush against the smooth, taut skin of the apple just before her teeth sink in with a soft crunch. She pauses, savoring the first burst of sweetness as her tongue sweeps across her lips catching a stray drop of juice.

What I would give to be that fucking drop of juice.

In an attempt to distract myself from my internal dialogue not helping the current situation growing in my pants, I take a bite of my own apple and move in close to her. I slowly place a kiss on her cheek, then her jaw, and finally the corner of her mouth. Just when I think I'm making progress, she raises the apple to her mouth and takes another bite. Not willing to give up, I look down and place another soft kiss on her shoulder. When she swallows her last bite I move back up, and kiss her jaw, noticing with each kiss more goosebumps tickle her skin. Just as I pull away to look into her eyes for permission before I kiss her for real, she quickly places her hand on the back of my head holding me close.

"Kiss me," she says with a soft smile.

I smile realizing at this moment, she is going to call all the shots, and I am fucking here for it. I press my lips to hers. It starts slow, but she quickly deepens the kiss, exploring my mouth with her tongue, until there is nothing soft about it. It becomes raw and hard and full of need, hot as fuck! I love that she takes what she wants from me. I have been on dates where girls hold back because they are worried about what people will think. I can tell, Ana doesn't give a shit. She knows what she wants and what she expects for herself, and demands it unapologetically. She made that perfectly clear at the diner when she put me in my place, and again right now, taking control. A strong woman who knows what she wants is hot.

Deciding to match her energy, I deepen the kiss, and our tongues dance. I quickly turn her and push her up against the tall tree stump, holding her in place with my hips. There is no way she can't tell just how much I am loving this kiss with how hard my dick is, and right now I don't care. Her hands move to my hair, tugging and pulling, and her right leg snakes around mine, at the ankle, pulling me into her even closer. With each kiss she lets out a heavy breath, and I feel like I'm in a goddamn dream! I have never had a kiss this raw and passionate, and bursting with energy. My hands, however, are dancing around in the air like a fucking idiot, trying to find a safe place to land. I roam the air around her body, moving from her back to her ass, back up to the nape of her neck, never actually making contact.

"Knox," she says on a heavy breath.

"Do not fucking say my name like that, Stitch. I only have so much control. Please, just- fuck. Don't say it with your voice like that," I chuckle trying to smother the flames brewing inside me.

She gives me a seductive smile.

"I just wanted to know why you were standing there like a kid dancing uncomfortably with his date in middle school. You're kind of killing the mood, I thought you'd have more game than that, you know as a fuckboy," she teases, nipping my bottom lip.

I raise my brow, pull her into me and lift her into my arms as she locks her ankles around me, I take her ass in both hands, deepening the kiss and pressing my hard length into her. She lets out a gasp, and I swallow the sound just as I hear talking on the other side of the trees. I slowly slide her down my front, pinning her once again between my hips and the tree stump as I slow the pace of the kiss, pull away and place one small peck on the tip of her nose.

Panting and not wanting too push to far, I say, "We need to get the fuck out of here before I get lost in you and we get caught. Plus Jack and Sally are up in about 45 minutes, let's go get a seat before it fills up." I slide my hand around hers and peel her off the tree leading her back to the festival.

She was silent for a few minutes and then put her hand out to stop me after her breathing had evened out.

"Knox, what was that, what you said to me back there?"

Fuck, too much!

"Ana, I'm sorry," I sigh. "I was just so, I don't know, that kiss." I take a breath. "It was amazing, and I was, I don't know, caught up, " She puts her finger to my lips to silence me.

"Knox, that's not what I meant. What you called me, what was that?"

"Stitch," I murmur, closing the distance between us and whispering in her ear, "I've been calling you that all day in my head, I didn't realize I said it out loud." My breath on the delicate skin just below her ear, causes a shiver to cross her neck. I press a tender, lingering kiss to her pulse point, feeling the rapid thrum beneath my lips. "I'm fucking broken right now, Anabelle," I confess, my voice rough and vulnerable. "But, spending time with you today … it's like you're helping to stitch me back together, piece by piece. I saw you last night, and you- I know it sounds fucking crazy, but trying to get your number gave me a glimpse of hope that I can be whole again. Today you made me forget just how fucking shattered I am."

I let my lips linger, brushing a slow, open-mouthed kiss against her neck making my cock jump to life once again. When I pull away, I immediately miss the heat of her skin. Her eyes meet mine, and in the charged silence, the space between us seems to hum with unspoken desire.

Today has been one of those days where hopelessness and self loathing overtake every single thought running through my head. There have been several times I have walked over to my nightstand, pulled out those little pills and debated falling to their magnetic pull. Knowing my future is unclear after having it written in the stars, is enough to take me under. I know I can't do this on my own, so I called my therapist after my doctor appointment last week and increased my in person sessions.

Today's session was exceptionally difficult because I cannot bring myself to come to terms with the fact baseball is not in the cards. This feeling is dark and consuming, and I have found myself actively grieving the loss of myself and who I have always known myself to be. Diving into that realization today was too much for me to digest so I've shoved it down.

Right now I am sitting on the couch, shifting my attention from the baseball game on the TV to the bottle of whiskey on the table and the familiar pills back in my pocket.

I grab the pills and set them next to the bottle, this familiar debate setting in when my attention shifts again to my phone as it vibrates in my pocket. When I pull it out, Ana's picture appears on the screen.

"Hey," I say, answering the phone.

"How was your session today?" she asks, jumping straight to the point.

"Ok," I say, not even convincing myself.

"I have something for you. Can I come over?" she asks.

"Of course, I'll send you the address again," I answered, relieved for the distraction.

"Good, but I'm outside the door," she laughs.

Ana has only been here one other time. She was at a bookstore the other day when we were on the phone, and when she told me the name of it, I realized it was the one around the corner. I met her in front of my building when she finished buying her books and we grabbed lunch.

Excited for the company I jump up and rush over to the door.

When I open the door she has a soft smile on her face and a tiny velvet bag hanging off her finger.

"What's that?" I question as I slide it off her finger.

"Open it."

"Come in," I say as I place a soft kiss on her forehead and then open the bag.

I pull out a small black ring. "Ana, we barely know each other," I tease.

She laughs "It's a fidget ring. I've noticed you tend to glide your fingers together when you are nervous or talk about things that are uncomfortable, and I know you had an appointment today, so I thought it would be a good time to give it to you. Maybe it can help you when you feel out of sorts."

"Thank you," I say in a bashful tone. "I'm not sure how you knew I needed this and you, but you have no idea how perfect your timing is."

"I guessed on the size, we can return it if it doesn't fit," she says and I slide it over my finger.

"It fits perfectly," I reassure her.

"Can I use your restroom? I drank way too much coffee," she asks.

"Yeah it's down the hall, first door on the left."

Just as the door to the bathroom closes, I remember the concerning buffet of substances scattered on the coffee table. I rush over and put it all away just as she emerges.

"Do you want company while you watch the game?" she asks, pointing to the TV.

"I would love company." Company is exactly what I need right now.

Ana pulls a blanket off the back of the couch and settles in next to me, cuddling into my side. It's amazing how perfectly she fits, it's like the curves of her body were made to fit with mine like the edges of two puzzle pieces.

As we sit and watch the game together, Ana asks questions about baseball as we watch, and it takes all of 30 seconds for me to realize she has not watched much baseball in her life. The dead giveaway is when she asks what quarter the game is in. I lean back on the couch, clutching my chest and feigning injury as if the question itself has wounded me, which makes her laugh. I love how invested she is in learning more about the game I love. And the bonus is she's cute when she's inquisitive, and a little furrow appears between her brows.

Maybe we can go to a game together.

Just then Ana moves and it causes the scent of her shampoo to circle around me and steal my thoughts. I love the flowery scent. I take one hand and brush it in soft repetitive strokes through her hair, and it causes her to settle into my side even more. My other hand is clasped in hers resting on my lap. She slowly unhooks our fingers and strikes them up and down the length of my thigh in soft long motions. The sensation sends a jolt of pleasure through my body awakening my dick and causing it to react. Ana eyes lower to the bulge building in my pants, and slowly crawls in my lap and straddles me. She begins to kiss my lips in soft pecks, gradually increasing the intensity as she slowly involves her entire mouth in the interaction. As each motion of her lips intensifies so does the rocking of her hips. Before I know it we are both rocking back and forth against each other wanting any friction the motion will offer. Due to the fact I chose sweats instead of jeans, Ana is able to slide over the entire length of my erection.

The more she rocks the more erratic her breathing becomes until she is fully panting, laying heavy breaths over each kiss. My breaths echo hers, as she continues to rock over me.

"Ana, wait," I say, trying to slow things down because watching her come undone has me on the brink of coming.

"Knox, please I'm so close." She shutters as her motions quicken.

So fucking hot.

I watch her as she reaches her climax on top of me, imagining what she would sound like with my dick inside her.

Her body goes limp just as her motions slow and her breathing slows, the sight sends me over the edge, my release coating the inside of my boxers.

After a few minutes of holding her close, I excuse myself to change. When I return she is cuddled up in the blanket, eyes heavy. I crawl in behind her and wrap my arms around her and we watch the rest of the game, like it's any typical night.

How the fuck did she know I needed her today? I wonder as my eyes become heavy and a calm I have been searching for falls over me.

Things between Ana and I are better than I could have ever imagined. We talk everyday and hang out as much as possible. The only downfall being I've had a constant raging hardon, and aside from the little over the clothes friction the other day, I've been left with only my hand as relief. Anabelle is on my mind all fucking day. Every day. The way she looks, the way she smells, the way her kisses fucking taste. I can't seem to get enough.

Standing here in the shower right now is no different. I just keep replaying tonight over and over, on loop in my brain. Our goodbye tonight was charged with intensity. Her lingering touch and the warmth of her body pressed against mine are playing on repeat. The way she looked at me with those sparkling blue eyes, so full of unspoken promises, and desire. Ana is reserved and with how hesitant she is to let people get too close, I don't want to push things too fast. I want everything that unfolds between us to be on her terms. She's too special to risk fucking this up, so I wait and rely heavily on my hand until I can round the bases with her.

I dropped her off at her apartment tonight, the engine of my Jeep still idling as the last traces of our heated make out session fade away. The interior is thick with the scent of fast food, and the smell of her shampoo, the heady mix enhanced by the lingering smell of her arousal.

We spent the day in a whirlwind of spontaneous adventures, driving aimlessly with no particular destination in mind, stuffing our faces with greasy burgers and fries. We found ourselves driving through various neighborhoods looking at Halloween decorations. We laughed over the ridiculousness of some of them as we passed, some elaborate, others hilariously tacky. Her infectious enthusiasm for the holiday made me smile.

After we'd had enough fast food and were stuffed to the brim, we wandered through a string of stores, gathering a variety of Halloween decorations, inspired by the homes we'd passed on our drive. She'd insisted no one could truly love Halloween without decking out their space, and I couldn't help but be swayed.

"Seriously, Knox," she said, holding up a string of purple lights with a playful grin. "You can't be a Halloween lover and not have a single Halloween decoration in your home. Your balcony needs to scream Halloween!"

I laughed, watching her excitement as she dragged me through the aisles of decorations. The day was perfect. And after sitting in the dim light of my Jeep with Ana's taste on my tongue and tits in my hands, I didn't want to let her go, but I have to be at the field early in the morning.

As she opened the car door and began to step out, I reached out, catching her hand gently. "Hey, Anabelle…"

She turned back to me, her eyes softening in the low light. "Yeah?"

I looked at her, struggling to find the right words. "Today was… fucking amazing. Who knew turning into a Halloween fanatic could be so much fun?"

Her smile grows, a mix of satisfaction and something deeper. "I had a great time too, Knox. You know, you're really starting to grow on me, with your willingness to allow me to force you to do shit, *especially* decorating for Halloween."

I chuckled, squeezing her hand lightly before letting go. "I guess I'm a convert now. I'll see you soon?"

"Maybe," she teased, leaning in for a quick kiss. It started gentle but quickly escalated into a promise of more, the kind of kiss that lingers in your mind long after it's over.

As she walked up to her apartment, I watched the silhouette of her body, with a heavy focus on her ass until she was safely inside. When she finally disappeared through her front door, I sat for a moment longer, trying to talk my dick down so I could focus and drive home.

Now that I'd secured my new job as the scoreboard operator for the Mountaineers, home is the second bedroom at Ethan's, finally allowing me to move out of my childhood bedroom at my parents'. My first paycheck comes in a few weeks, but I paid Ethan out of my graduation money for the first month's rent.

Ana and I spent three days, both in person and over text looking for baseball-related jobs I could apply for. One morning, I bit the bullet and applied for the scoreboard operator position that had occupied many of our conversations. I guess if I can't play baseball, spending the off season learning how to watch it for a living is the next best thing. Ana never pushed, she just talked through the pros and cons and encouraged me to do something to try to fill the void developed by not playing. Her way of helping me move past what I thought my future was supposed to be.

Just another loop of the thread.

As I walk through the front door, I'm relieved Ethan is still out at some concert. I put all of the decorations in my room and walked to the bathroom to turn on the shower. I undress while the water heats up, and as the steam builds around me, my thoughts as usual drift to Ana.

Now I'm standing in the shower, thinking about Anabelle, and how good she looks. Fuck! All I can think about is being with her. I can't help but picture her movements, fluid and deliberate, as she walked through the store. It is causing an almost primal excitement. My imagination goes wild, and I envision our first time together with the most vivid detail. I imagine what it would be like to have her lean into me, a promise of more in her posture, a silent invitation.

I can't help but picture her back arched into my mattress as I worship her, the curves of her body accentuated by her arched position. The idea of her here, in my space, making it come alive with her presence, stirs a longing way beyond a physical desire.

Those thoughts are all it takes and I'm hard once again. I squeeze some body wash in my right hand and slowly start moving it up and down my shaft squeezing with just a little more pressure as I get to the head. A flash of her lips, soft and slick from the lip balm she is always applying pops in my head. I imagine them slowly sliding down my dick until I meet the back of her throat. I imagine them stretched out in a perfect "o" as I fill them, her bright blue eyes staring back up at me as I empty myself down her throat. I have to use my left hand to hold myself up on the shower wall in front of me, as I empty myself all over the shower floor. But as I stand here panting, I feel anything but satisfied.

Fuck. I can't wait to see her again.

Ana

"KNOX, I DON'T UNDERSTAND, how do you keep track of so much happening at one time?" I ask with a chuckle as Knox wraps his arm around me cuddling me tight to his side.

We have been watching a baseball game on tv in Knox's living room for the last hour so Knox can "sharpen his eye" before he starts his new job, and despite the hours I have spent trying to learn it, I'm still so confused.

"I've lived and breathed this game since I was old enough to pick up a ball. This game was my first true love." His smile is intoxicating. "Fuck yeah!" He shouts as he gently slides out from our embrace and stands, pumping his fist in the air.

"He got an RBI, right?" I ask. "Even though they got him out, the run still counts."

Knox stares at me dumbfounded for a second. "Shit, that's so hot. You learned baseball for me."

"I tired, but that's really all I remember."

"Baseball is a complex, Stitch. I'm impressed."

"So, what happens now?" I ask, confusion still rattling my brain, eventhough I try to conceal it.

"The next batter comes up to hit, and they keep going until there are three outs, right now there are two."

"The camera keeps moving. It's hard to track what's happening." I sigh.

"Fuck yeah!" He says again, sitting back down and cuddling me in close.

I'm not quite sure what happened, but the look in his eyes feels like pure magic-so breathtaking and rare. Something I wish I could preserve and carry with me.

Even though I'm no baseball expert, I can see why he loves this sport so much. It's technical and strategic, just like him. Based on the look of admiration in his eyes, I know why his injury was so devastating for him.

"It's hard to get the full picture of the game on TV. Sometimes, it's a little boring." He looks down at me from where he stands, "Do you want to go to a game with me? Seeing it in person is so much better." The smile spreading across his face is so damn cute, I could never say no.

"That would be amazing," I smile.

When Knox asked me to go to a game with him, this is not what I imagined. We are sitting in the grass under the shade of a beautiful maple tree watching 12 year olds play little league.

"This is the full experience?" I ask.

"Hell yeah it is. You want to get immersed in the world and love of baseball, this is the best place to see it. Up close, the chants the players repeat feeling like surround sound," He smiles. "Back here, you will get to watch the raw joy that comes from all the firsts. The first in park homerun, the first double play, passion that materializes in tears and puffed chests, like they're a bunch of tough guys when they get disappointed by their mistakes. It's magic, Stitch. There is no better place to start your baseball journey."

"I love how much you love this game, Knox." I bring his hand to my mouth and lay a gentle kiss on his knuckles. "Have you ever coached? I feel like you would be an amazing coach," I ask.

"No, but I love little league so much and love the fundamentals of the game, I'd love to someday. My dream is to work with kids," he chuckles at a few moms in the stands nearby. " You want to see a love for the game? Raw passion? You won't see anything more unhinged than a mom in the stands who believes she saw the call better than the ump."

I look in their direction, mouth agape. "I can't imagine acting that way."

"That's because you're made to be a coach's wife," he says with a cheeky smile pointing at one of the moms sitting by herself at the end of the fence as far away from the stands as possible. She has her shades on, feet up on the fence, watching the game intently while she sips on her straw.

"How do you know she's the coach's wife?" I ask.

"Because they're all the same. It demands an almost superhuman strength of character to remain unmoved by the chorus of criticism aimed at the coach, their husband, but instead offer a genuine smile, and to simply be present for their child, because it's all that really matters."

"You think she has water in her cup?" I ask.

"Fuck no. There is most definitely alcohol in her cup," he laughs.

He looks down at our fingers intertwined and brings them to his lips, mimicking the kiss I just placed on his. When his lips make contact with my flesh, I see it in vivid detail.

Knox standing on the side of the field, clipboard in hand, spitting seeds in the dirt, me in a chair with my feet propped up on the fence, stealing glances of each other as often as we can, until a slender frame takes the plate- the perfect mix of us.

Knox squeezes my hand.

I think he can see it too.

I'm standing in front of my closet, once again, not knowing what in the hell to wear. I'm staring at rows of clothes with a mix of excitement and nerves. Knox and I have spent a lot of time together, but this date feels different, planned, special. Plus it's my birthday, and Knox is surprising me, adding another layer to the nerves. Since I met Knox, we have spent more time together than apart, going on hikes, grabbing lunch and coffee, having movie nights, with a little too much over the clothes action. My heart flutters at the thought as I pull out a dress, a deep blue with long sleeves and the length hitting just above the ankle. It's a perfect fall maxi dress, one that looks like the *right* thing to wear on a date. It's not my usual attire, but it looks hot.

As I slip the dress on, it feels unfamiliar, the fabric is cold against my skin, and has me feeling slightly out of my comfort zone. I bought it for a bridal shower I attended, and it's been gathering dust in the back of my closet since. Walking out of the closet, I catch my reflection in the mirror and pause. The dress hugs me in all the right places, but I feel out of my skin. "You've got this," I whisper offering myself a little pep talk, hoping it will help. Still, part of me is wondering if I should opt for something a little more *me*.

I applied more makeup than usual, and in my reflection in the mirror all focus goes straight to my eyes. I notice how the smokey bronze eyeshadow I smeared on makes the blue stand out, way more than usual. The precise line of black liner is giving them a subtle cat-eye effect, topping the look off with thick lashes created by layers of mascara, making me look dopy and doe eyed. My cheeks have a touch of blush for a natural flush, and my lips are painted a bold red I stole from Blake's room, a color I never wear, making them appear fuller and succulent.

I hear a knock at the door. Shit, Knox is here. Grabbing my clutch, also not my usual accessory of choice, I hesitate before opening the door, taking a deep breath. My nerves swirling around inside me like a silent hurricane only amplified by the dumb ass dress and face I don't recognize.

I finally open the door, and Knox's breath hitches, "Shit, you look amazing. That dress, fuck, Ana" His eyes are roaming my body, and when he gets to my eyes, they are soft, they have transformed from desire to *concern.*

"You, you ok?" he asks me as his eyes roam up my body again, but this time I am aware of my hands tugging at my dress, and my weight shifting from one foot to the other. Where I am usually confident and collected, right now I'm sure I seem anything but.

I nod in a silent response and I reach to grab his hand. He takes it gently, but instead of leading me out the door, he steps into my apartment, and closes it. He backs me against the door and leans in bearing all of his weight on his forearm just above my head. Placing his forehead against mine, he whispers, "What's wrong?"

"I thought it would be nice to wear makeup and something out of the norm, but it just doesn't feel right," I sigh.

"I mean you look hot, Stitch, but you look hot in everything. If it's not comfortable, you can change, we have plenty of time." The nickname he uses for me sends a little shiver of delight up my spine, knowing it is something special, just for me. He is still leaning in, and the green of his eyes is so bright.

"I don't know where we are going, so I wanted to make sure I was dressed for any occasion, but I'm not loving it," I breathe out.

"Are surprises not your thing?" he asks.

"I don't know," I say honestly. "I've never had one."

"Well in that case, I'll keep it a surprise so you can decide for yourself when it's all said and done, but if you want to change I can help you pick out something that will fit the atmosphere of where we are going." His smile is so genuine as he waits for my response.

"That would be amazing, I feel like I have paint on my face and this long dress feels too formal." I breathe a sigh of relief as he grabs my hand and leads me down the hallway to the bedrooms stopping just before the first door.

"It's that one," I say gesturing to the door a little further down the hall.

His movements are gentle yet deliberate. As soon as we walk through the door, he places a soft kiss on my lips and gestures towards the dress. "May I?" he asks.

I nod my head giving him silent approval. He bends down and grabs the hem of the dress, and slowly pulls it over my head. Peppering me with kisses in his path, his touch is tender, devoid of expectation, yet intimate. His fingers brush lightly against my skin, sending shivers down my spine. My breath hitches and my core heats as his knuckles create lazy paths across my skin, leaving goosebumps in their wake. As the dress comes over my head, I feel my nipples pebble under my bra. Knox uses the curve of the index finger he placed under my chin to pull me towards him, and places a soft kiss on my lips.

Slowly he retreats to the bathroom, I hear the water turn on and then off again, it takes a moment before he reappears in the doorway, with a damp towel in his hand. He glides towards me with fluid motion, as if he's sliding across my room on ice rather than the carpet covering the floor. When he approaches me, he gently pushes me onto the bed, so I am sitting right at the foot. Placing a hand on my thigh, he kneels before me, and he brushes soft kisses up my arms to my neck, and when he reaches my face, he begins to wipe the makeup off with a softness that feels like a whisper against my skin. The warmth of the towel creates a soothing sensation as it melds with the cool air filling the room. I close my eyes, wondering how he is so in tune with what I need after only a few weeks.

After every ounce of makeup has been removed from my face, and I feel more like myself, Knox leans over and places the rag on my nightstand, switching it out for my lip balm and face lotion. Handing them to me, he stands us up, places his hand on the small of my back and motions me towards my closet. I apply a small amount of lotion to my face and set it on the dresser and then do the same with the lip balm before I start searching for the perfect outfit.

"The place we are going to is casual, yet sophisticated," he whispers in my ear from where he stands behind me.

I turn around for a moment to really take him in, trying to match the items I choose to the vibe he is giving off. He is wearing tan chinos with a white button up with the sleeves rolled to show off his impressive forearms. He has a thin dark grey Carhartt vest and matching leather sneakers.

Casual, yet sophisticated.

"What are you doing?" he asks.

"Trying to match your vibe," I say, turning back to my clothes. I pull various articles of clothing off the hangers and go to hang them over my arm when he intercepts my hand, bringing it to his mouth and laying a kiss across my knuckles, and then slowly takes the clothes from me and carries them back into my bedroom. I follow as he lays each item on the edge of my bed with precision. When he is finished I reach for the knit turtleneck shirt on the bed, but he stops me. Knox doesn't say a word, but shakes his head at me, signaling me not to touch them. I return my hand to my side and watch him, his silence mixed with the devoted look in his eyes is making me heat inside. How can he say so much, communicate so much without actually saying a single word? This interaction is laced with intimacy, yet it's clear sex is not his intention.

He turns slowly, pulling me into his embrace, "You are absolute perfection." His lips press against mine, his tongue slowly dances across mine as I open my mouth. He pulls back, pressing a soft kiss to my forehead, and then picks up the knit top and slides it over my head. He dresses me with the same care and attention he had shown in undressing me. Adjusting my shirt with tender precision. There is something romantic about the way he keeps his eyes locked on mine as he watches me slide my jeans on and when he reaches out to fasten the button, my heart flutters. I have never been so turned on by someone putting my clothes *on* before, but as his knuckles brush my warm skin, heated by this exchange, I have to clench my thighs needing any semblance of pressure to release the throb of my clit. When he's done securing the button on my jeans, he looks me in the eyes, his voice a gentle whisper as he hands me my ankle boots. "You look incredible." His voice is full of gravel, pure sex.

Holy shit!

I turn to the mirror admiring my cropped wide-leg jeans styled with a tucked in fitted knit turtleneck and ankle boots.

My vibe matches his perfectly.

Knowing Knox appreciates me for me, has only made me more eager to go out with him. After I place the finishing touches on my new look, and we conclude our heated makeout session, we finally head down to Knox's Jeep, on our way to our chosen date spot.

Knox planned the perfect outing, knowing how much I have been wanting to visit the new winery in town. It's nestled in the rolling hills, tucked away in a secluded valley, offering a serene escape from the world.

As we drive up the winding roads, the landscape opens up to reveal lush vineyards and a charming stone building. It looks just like the picture on their social media page, and truly like it just popped straight out of a movie.

Knox guides me to the spacious deck, where a small table is set with a bottle of wine and two glasses, shimmering in the light. He pulls out my chair, and brushes a kiss across my cheek. After he sits across from me, he pours the wine, its rich, ruby hue mimicking the warmth I feel deep in my core. The clinking of the bottle as it brushes against the rim of my glass creates a chime that seems to blend with the music drifting up from the concert on the lawn. Knox sets the bottle down on the table and looks at me, his eyes full of lust.

"Are you going to pour yourself a glass?" I ask

"No, they have beer. I really don't like wine."

"Then why did you bring me to a winery?"

"Because today is all about you, Stitch," he replies simply.

We spend the next several hours listening to music, and exploring the grounds. Our conversations punctuated by the occasional burst of laughter, more uninhibited due to my subtle buzz from the wine. As we stroll through the vineyard, I sample various wines set up at tables across the venue. Each sip sparks lively conversation, and I even convince Knox to take the tiniest sip of my wine since he doesn't seem to be enjoying the beer he's nursing. I'm not sure I've even seen him take a sip.

He must be worried about the drive home.

He didn't enjoy the wine any more, given the sour face he made when barely a drop coated his lip.

We casually make our way up a small hill to a tasting room. The winery's charm surrounds the building, but the tasting room's panoramic view of the rolling hills creates an impressive view. We wander through the wine barrels, share stories, and indulge in flirtatious banter. The hum of the soft music filling the space adds to our relaxed and carefree exploration as we approach the back corner of the tasting room.

"Knox, this is amazing. I can officially say I love surprises. Thank you." He gives me a soft smile and reaches for my free hand. "This wine is delicious," I say.

"I can think of something that probably tastes way better than the wine." His words are sultry as they leave his lips, full of insinuation. My stomach erupts in butterflies from the thought of Knox between my legs.

He laces his fingers with mine, occasionally leaning down to pepper small sensual kisses on my shoulder. As we continue our walk along the grounds we stumble upon a secluded spot tucked behind a small cliff. The world seems to have faded away as we stand here, caught up in the moment, just the two of us. The sounds of the concert are a dim hum in the distance, the perfect background music. We can faintly hear the sounds of the music and people singing along, making it clear we are truly alone and no one will know we are hidden back here. This idea is only escalating the tension between us, anticipation of the what-ifs swirling around in my head, causing me to once again clench my thighs in an attempt to relieve the building pressure.

Knox reaches out, gently brushing a hair from my face. His fingers linger, tracing the curve of my cheek, a shiver running through me. We have been here before, secluded from the world. Our eyes lock, and in an instant, the shimmering heat between us ignites.

He pulls me closer, his hand resting on my waist, and I tilt my head up, to give him better access to my neck as he trails up my jaw with kisses. My breath hitching in my throat. Our lips meet in a heated kiss, full of passion and longing. Knox is intense, a mix of tenderness and urgency. I respond immediately, my hands finding their way to the nape of his neck, fingers tangling in his hair.

I press myself against him, his body seeping into mine, grinding against my core. I can feel his hard length press against my clit, creating a pressure I have been craving. The kiss deepens, and I can taste the faint flavor from the sip of wine on his lips, causing a small moan to escape my lips.

Time seems to have stopped, as we lose ourselves in each other. Knox's hands roam up my back, pulling me even closer, as he tugs the collar of my turtleneck loose, so he can pepper it with kisses. His motions are much more precise, practiced, and deliberate compared to the last time we were here, in this situation. Each motion is a silent promise.

Without a word, he grabs my hand and we move past the cliff to an area offering even more privacy.

"Let's get out of here," I say.

"Who says we have to leave?" he responds as he pulls me in close.

"Knox, we're in public," I laugh.

"That's the thrill." He smiles. "But if you–"

I put my finger over his mouth to silence him. "I'm just surprised, that's all. But I love surprises now, remember?" I say giving him a nod of approval.

As nervous as I am to be this vulnerable in a public space, the "thrill" so to speak is adding to the growing pressure building within me. Knox and I have been play-ful and somewhat reserved, only engaging in over the clothes touches and passionate kisses, but right now I don't have the composure needed for the long walk out of here and the drive home. I want whatever it is he is offering, and the idea he is so needy for me, that he too can't wait, is making my judgment spiral.

Knox moves in front of me, placing one hand on my hip, and one at my jawline, leaning in for a soft supple kiss. It starts slow, but builds with the tension. I move my hand to the hem of his shirt and slide a finger underneath. He instantly stops my hand with his and shakes his head.

Then he mimics my action, sliding the pad of his index finger beneath the hem of my shirt as he slowly untucks just the corner. I decide to mimic his response and place my hand on his, but again he stops me and shakes his head.

Deciding to change my approach, I raise up on my tip toes and place a soft kiss on his neck. He lets out a soft moan and then pulls away.

"Stitch, I want this to be all about you. Please, let me show you just how perfect I think you are," he says, pulling at the back of his neck.

I lean back against the side of the small cliff letting go of all my inhibitions and submitting to his request. I want nothing more than to see myself through his eyes.

Knox kisses my neck and slowly skirts his fingers over my jeans applying feather-like pressure right between my legs. He dances his fingers lazily over my jeans and then slowly brings his hand up to the zipper and begins unzipping them. All the while he is kissing me, worshiping the warm skin of my neck, earlobes, lips. He slowly slips his hand beneath my jeans and panties and runs his fingers through my drenched slit. After laying a few circles of his finger around my clit, he removes his hand and slides his fingers into his mouth, licking them clean. His eyes roll back in his head and my thighs heat.

He then bends down, and begins sliding my jeans down and then drops to his knees. Without hesitation, he pulls my panties to the side and his mouth is on me, running his tongue along my opening, already soaked from all the built anticipation. The cool feeling of his lip ring brushing across my skin is a stark contrast to the heat built up inside me and sends shivers down my spine. He slowly slides his tongue inside. The motion is gentle, sending an intense throb to my clit. He must sense it, because right then he moves his thumb to my clit, placing the perfect amount of pressure.

He looks up at me, eyes wide. "You have a piercing," he says, more of a statement than a question.

"Vertical hood," I respond with a smirk.

"That is so fucking hot," he whispers, almost sounding like a low growl, then returns his attention. "You taste *so* good Ana, better than I could have ever imagined."

This man. I think and my head tilts back and a ragged breath escapes my mouth.

He licks at my clit with hunger and precise long motions, my legs quivering with each swipe of his tongue. Between the feel of his hot breath on my pussy and the fear of someone catching us, it doesn't take me long to reach my peak. I feel the familiar sensation of pressure building between my legs, and a loud moan escapes my mouth. Knox reaches up to stifle it, placing his hand over my mouth.

I come with a force I have never before experienced. My body trembles, and a faint sweat breaks out over my skin. When I finally come down from the high, Knox is standing there smiling, his mouth wet from my arousal, each droplet reflecting the vibrant hues of the fading sun. The bulge pressing against his pants is unmistakable, and I find myself running my tongue along my lower lip, mouth watering as I stare.

"Happy birthday, Stitch," he says with a devilish grin as he wipes his mouth.

Today, March 1

"Drops of rain they fall all over"
-Blink 182

Knox

I HOLD HER HAND the entire ambulance ride to the hospital, refusing to let go. I run my fingers over the fidget ring Ana gave me as I watch her intently. The smooth outer ring gliding over the metal band lying beneath. Ana floats in and out of consciousness, and every time she wakes the same few sentences leave her lips and make my stomach curl.

"Knox, he can't see me like this," she pleads.

"Please, Knox, tell him how much I love him."

"Where is Riker?"

"RIKER!"

She screams his name, over and over, each time she comes to. It's breaking me apart, snapping each thread she put into place. I'm selfish and all I want to hear at this moment is how she has missed being with me, and wants to be with me… forever!

As we arrive at the hospital, the paramedics' movements quicken. My phone is ringing like crazy. Ana's parents and brother keep calling for updates. I had the paramedics call her dad, I couldn't find the words to make the call myself. Now, it just keeps ringing on repeat, I can't pull my attention away from her, not now! When the doors slam open, there is a team of doctors on the other side. They quickly pull her out of the ambulance, me chasing behind them. Once we're inside, everything is distorted. Suddenly they rush her through the double doors at the end of a long hallway marked with a bright red line drawn on the floor, "*STAFF ONLY.*" The words stop me in my tracks, but they keep going with Ana down the long hallway before me.

My heart aches as I watch them fade through the small window on the door.

I wait in the emergency waiting room for what feels like hours, and now she's in surgery. I haven't gotten an update for what seems like an eternity. I just keep telling myself: *no news is good news.*

Right?

Fall, Three Years Ago

"I'm not in the scene
I think I'm falling asleep
But then all that it means is I'll
Always be dreaming of you"
-Blink 182

Knox

A NA AND I HAVE both been busy the last few weeks, and I wanted to focus all of my time and attention on planning the perfect birthday trip to the winery for Ana, so the Halloween decorations we bought are still sitting in bags on my bedroom floor. Tonight, she is coming over to decorate. I ordered Chinese for dinner from the place down the street and have a few Halloween movies ready to go. We have already seen my favorite, The Nightmare Before Christmas, on our first date- so the first one we're going to watch is hers: Hocus Pocus.

The doorbell rings, and I open the door... fuck me. I can't even look at her face because my eyes go immediately to her perky tits on display in a thin, almost see through sweatshirt hanging off her right shoulder. The curve of the top of her right tit peeks out of the neckline hanging low on one side. She has on a tiny ass low cut sports bra, baggy sweats, and her hair is pulled into one of those messy buns on top of her head. I bite my lower lip, sucking in my lip ring.

"You are such a perverted dick sometimes, Knox, I'm in sweats," she says with a slight giggle, rolling her eyes, as pushes past me making her way into my apartment.

"I'm not staring at the sweats, Stitch," I say as I close the door and make my way towards her. "I'm staring at those perfect tits of yours, but the sweats, those are an added bonus," I lower my voice and place my hands on her hips, thumbs sliding into the waistband. "Great for easy access," I whisper in her ear. Then kiss down the side of her neck ending with one soft kiss just at her jawline.

"Mmmm," she whimpers as she drapes her arms around my neck.

Just then the doorbell rings, and I pull away. "Guess it's time to eat," I say with a smile, wiggling my eyebrows and all I get from her in return is a blank stare. "Nothing, No response to that?" I ask as I close the door after grabbing the food from the delivery driver.

"Hey, let's put the food in the oven to stay warm while we decorate," she says, opening packages on the kitchen table ignoring me completely.

"You're no fucking fun," I say as I honor her request and place the take-out bags in the oven to stay warm. "But we're not decorating this balcony, Ethan will kick my ass," I announce. There is a small balcony window in each of our rooms that slides open with a little ledge to stand on, but not big enough for furniture. Instead of an iron fence like the main balcony, it has one railing across the top, a small gap, and then a wall lined with siding to give more privacy. "We can decorate mine. It's the perfect size for all of the things we got."

"I didn't see another balcony when I walked up," she says, confused.

"Well technically it's called a Juliet Balcony, but it just sounds really dumb to me, so to me it's just a balcony."

"Are you talking about the giant flower box-looking thing outside your window in your bedroom?" she laughs.

"It's a balcony, okay? Just help me grab all of this shit, Stitch, and I'll show you," I say with a playful huff.

"Wow, fancy," she jokes, pausing for effect. Then she smiles and continues, "Actually, this is pretty awesome, Knox." She moves around the space pointing as she says, "I would have a chair right here so I could read and look outside. I'd cuddle up in a blanket, put a small table here, with a candle, and any time it rains, I would sit here all day."

As she talks to me, she starts pulling the decorations out of the bag. When she starts to place the decorations I can't help but watch. I watch her drape the lights across the railing, and the sight is even better than I imagined. Every movement she makes is fluid and deliberate, her concentration evident in the way her brow furrows slightly. The soft glow from the string lights casts a warm, inviting light over her, making her look like she belongs right here, decorating my balcony.

I sit on a stool I grabbed from the kitchen, positioning myself where I can see every detail. I hand her each decoration, carefully trying to make sure she gets exactly what she needs without breaking her rhythm. My focus is laser-sharp, unable to look away from her ass as she works.

Each time she bends at the waist to reach the railing, her ass turns into the perfect heart shape, a mouth watering curve that makes my breath catch. I find myself appreciating how the lights accentuate her every movement, how she seems to naturally embody the Halloween spirit we're creating together. It's both captivating and intoxicating.

I can't keep to myself any longer. I need to be close to her. My patience snaps, and I find myself standing right behind her, reaching around to hand her each decoration from there. The proximity brings a new level of intimacy. I'm close enough to feel the warmth of her body and smell the faint, sweet scent of her perfume mingling with the crisp autumn air. The combination ignites my senses.

As I hand her each piece, my fingers brush against her hand, sending a jolt of electricity straight to my cock. Every touch, every shared glance, feels loaded with a promise that's too strong to ignore. I watch her shoulders as she feels my presence behind her, a slight tension in her posture building.

"Need anything else?" I ask, my voice low, almost a murmur.

She turns her head slightly, enough to meet my eyes over her shoulder. The look she gives me is soft but filled with heat. "Just a little *more…*" she says playfully as she subtly pushes her ass against my dick. "Ummm… a few more lights." A playful grin spreads across her face, her voice full of suggestion, making my pulse quicken.

Our fingers brush again as I hand her another strand of lights, the contact lingering just a moment longer than necessary. The air between us crackles with an electric charge and it feels as real as the decorations we're hanging.

"Why do you love decorating for Halloween so much?" I ask, trying to distract myself from the boner forming in my pants.

"My grandpa Scott was my person. I spent every second with him I could, and his love for decorating and celebrating life's smallest moments was unmatched. He used to tell me, '*You only get one life Ana, you might as well decorate it. 'Every second is worth celebrating, no matter how small,*' and he lived that exact sentiment in all aspects of his life. He loved fiercely and every occasion was cause for celebration. So I guess, decorating, for any occasion, makes me feel close to him now that he's gone."

"Sounds like he was an amazing man, I wish I could have met him." I place a small kiss on her shoulder.

"He was the best," she whispers as she continues to add decorations to the small space.

As she continues to work, I'm mesmerized by the way she moves, how she transforms the balcony with her presence. The simple act of decorating becomes something more, a shared experience that feels intimate, and because my dick's still hard, full of filthy potential. The way she bends and stretches, the way her laughter dances through the air, it all draws me in.

Her ass looks so incredible in her sweats. "Fuck, Stitch," I speak in a hushed tone just loud enough for her to hear, she peeks over her shoulder and gives me a devilish grin. I reach out to grab it, needing the smallest amount of contact, but she swats my hand away. Instead, I pepper little kisses and nips with my teeth along her neck and down her arms as I hand her each decoration, hoping to break through her composed exterior.

I'm not sure how much time has passed while I'm lost in the intoxicating sight of her, her ass shifting with every movement, her unique scent, the memory of her skin lingering in my mouth from our earlier kisses. All I know is the next time I snap back to reality, my balcony has been transformed into a Halloween masterpiece.

Ana has truly outdone herself. The railing is enhanced with Jack Skellington lights twinkling with an eerie charm. A three-tiered pumpkin sits proudly in one corner, its carved faces glowing softly. Tiny purple and orange twinkling lights are strung across the door frame, casting a festive, whimsical glow. Little bats dangle from strings, fluttering gently in the doorway as if they're alive.

Her hair, now a bit disheveled from the work, frames her face in soft little waves that have fallen from her bun. The faint scent of pumpkin spice from the air freshener she added and her own unique scent, blend in the air, creating an intoxicating mix drawing me in even more. I can't help but admire her work, and how she's become the centerpiece of it all.

I let out a low whistle, not sure what else to say, taking in the scene before me. "Wow," I finally manage to say, the word barely scraping the surface of my awe. "This is fucking incredible… You said it would look amazing, and you've definitely delivered," I say, stepping closer, feeling the warmth of the lights and her presence heat me. "Thank you." I pull her into me tighter and press my lips to hers for another kiss.

She lets herself fall into me, deepening the kiss, slowly walking me backwards into my room. When we are all the way back in, she slowly turns away from me and slides the balcony door closed.

"I don't want to be the evening soundtrack for all your neighbors," she voices flirtatiously.

When she turns back around she crosses her arms across the front of her body, grabbing the hem of her sweatshirt in both hands, and slowly starts peeling it off over her head, her eyes never leaving mine. As she inches towards me, my breath hitches and I grow harder with every step she takes. With her final step she peels the black sports bra off and drops it to the floor. She looks at me and nods, giving her permission, and I bend down and take one of her nipples in my mouth, biting the pebbled flesh and following it with a soft lick across the skin to dull the sting. She moans and arches into me. With that small invitation, I bend slightly farther at the waist, snaking both of my hands around her ass, resting my hands just inside her upper thighs, lifting her off the ground. She wraps her arms around my neck, and her legs around my waist, pulling me in closer to her breasts, and I kiss them up and down as I navigate over to my bed and slowly lower her down.

When I climb on top of her, she pulls my shirt over my head, and when I lay down to kiss her, the feeling of our hot skin coming together breaks any resolve I have, and I think it broke hers too.

Every motion that follows is frantic, not calculated the way I imagined this going. I wanted to take my time. I wanted to worship her. I wanted to memorize every inch of her body. Instead I'm carnal, kissing and biting her skin, both of our hands are everywhere all at once. We are shedding clothes faster than I can register, and before I know it we are both completely naked.

Somewhere along the way we flipped over and she's straddling me, hovering just above me, kissing my neck, and biting my ear.

I push her back so she is sitting on my thighs. Without a word I pause and take her in, just for a second. There are no words to describe her. She is perfection. Her breasts are tear dropped with soft caramel nipples sitting directly in the center. Unable to resist, I run my hands over her skin tracing each curve and dip of her body. Instantly in love with the way her skin feels against mine, the softness of her stomach and the way her ass fills my hands as I slide them around the back of her body, just the perfect amount to bounce around. The thought makes my mouth water.

Fuck.

I sit up pushing her onto her back, wanting a better look. The silver of her piercing glistens in her arousal, like shards of stardust with a dazzling, ethereal sparkle, and I can't help but lick my lips at the sight. I move up her body slowly, so I am hovering over her, my hands on the bed caging her in. I kiss her neck, and then kiss her chest in between her breasts, moving to take one nipple into my mouth and quickly releasing it with a pop.

"Knox," she whimpers.

"I told you what would happen if you said my name like that," I challenge. As I look at her, she smirks. She said that on purpose.

"I thought I'd call your bluff. I thought you were a big talker," she says.

"I mean what I say, Ana. Don't say my name if you're not ready to have it fall off your lips all night."

I move my hand down her body and slide one finger through the wetness pooling between her legs and circle her clit adding soft pressure, pushing the bottom silver ball of her piercing into her clit. Then, without warning, I push the same finger deep inside her, and she gasps.

"Fuuuck, Ana," I moan. "You're so wet, so warm."

"Knox," she shudders, dragging my name out making clear eye contact, this time void of a smirk.

Taking it as an invitation, I pick up the pace pushing and pulling my finger in and out of her as I move my lips down, tracing her body with soft teasing kisses, until I'm finally face to face with her beautiful pussy. I begin laying long licks across her clit, and with each motion, my tongue plays with the little ball and hits her in just the right spot. She rakes her fingers through my hair and tugs, moving her body from side to side like she's trying to run away from the sensation, while pushing deeper into it at the same time. "Where the fuck do you think you're going baby? I'm not done with you," I demand as I remove my finger and use both hands to bring her back straight and pin her down.

"Please!" she groans in frustration.

"Please what, Ana? If you want something, baby, you have to fucking say it."

She looks me right in the eyes, "I want you to stop talking to me, stop telling me what to do, and get back between my legs."

"Like this?" I question, slamming two fingers inside her.

"Yes," she moans.

As I slide my fingers in and out, I use my other hand to spread her open, watching my fingers disappear inside her. With her spread open, I push my tongue against her clit watching her writhe against the pressure. Her walls clench around my fingers as her knees imprison my head from both sides and she finds her release. When she finally comes down, I slide my tongue along her slit from bottom to top wanting to taste every drop of what I have done to her. She shakes as I cross her clit. As her breathing starts to even out, she sits up, pushing me onto my back. I prop myself up on my elbows and without breaking eye contact, she slowly makes her way down my body, leaving a trail of soft kisses as she does, until she's staring at my dick.

"Mmmmm," is all I hear before she starts sliding her tongue up my length as she licks it from balls to tip, my eyes rolling back in my head as I drop down on the bed. She slowly takes me into her mouth, a little at first, sliding me in just below the tip, before sliding me back out. She works me like a pro, her mouth moving in perfect rhythm before she slides down quickly taking my cock all the way to the back of her throat. When I feel the walls of her throat tighten around me, it's all I can do to keep myself from losing control. Suddenly she pulls me out of her mouth completely and places long slow licks up my shaft before circling the head just once.

"Fuck yes," I moan, drawing out my words as if doing so will let me savor this sensation a little longer.

I feel her mouth coming off my dick and can feel her adjusting herself on the bed. Soon after, I feel warmth radiating my tip and slowly spreading as I open my eyes and prop back up on my elbows watching as she slides me inside her. I watch my dick disappear inch by inch until all I can see is where we are connected. My mouth opens wide with a deep breath, but nothing comes out.

"Oh shit, yes," she says as she starts to move up and down. I force myself to pull my head back up not wanting to miss a single thing. I watch her move up and down, extending and bending her knees each time she slides me in and out. Just as her breath turns from slow long pants to short erratic puffs, she slams down onto me, but instead of moving up and down, she is grinding into me from side to side, circling her hips, keeping me deep inside her. The friction of her piercing against my skin creates little goosebumps over her skin like flecks of glitter in the light casting from my balcony through the window.

Her taking control is the hottest fucking thing I have ever seen.

"Ana," I say barely above a whisper.

She is lost in her own release, her walls tightening around me as she calls my name.

"Ana, I'm… Ana!" I repeat, as I sit up trying to slide out of her. She places her hands on my shoulders and rocks even harder, her breath hitching, legs trembling at my sides. Then she crumbles down on top of me, as I feel my dick jerk with three quick movements, following with my own release.

Afterwards, we just lay here, her in my arms, still on top of me. For a few minutes we just listen to each other's breath as they even back out, then I slowly roll her on her back. I slide out of her, quickly taking my shirt and placing it between her legs to catch my release as it flows out of her, and place a soft kiss to her lips. I run to the en suite bathroom, cupping my balls as I run, Ana giggles. I turn on the water, and wait for it to heat up before placing a washrag beneath it. After I wring it out, I make my way back to the bed, using my free hand to spread her legs open, and as her knees hit the bed, I slowly run the warm cloth over her opening, cleaning her as I place soft kisses to her shoulder.

"Thank you," she says with a soft smile.

Eventually we get dressed, reheat our Chinese food and watch Hocus Pocus, as planned. I fall asleep on the couch somewhere around the time the witches enter the graveyard and fly in the air on brooms and a vacuum.

I wake up the next morning to the sound of Ethan making coffee in the kitchen. When I open my eyes and see a dark long lock of hair draped over my arm and Ana snuggled into my chest on the couch, I take a deep breath, close my eyes and lay there taking in the flowery scent of her hair. I'm beginning to realize trying to fill a void won't solve any of my problems. When you replace something old with something new, it never feels the same, and always seems to leave you wanting what you had. I need to find the same love I have for baseball in something new. Baseball has become my past, it's time to find my future. I find myself dozing off as my mind wanders, and before I know it, I'm back asleep.

When Ana and I finally wake up, we decide to take a shower, which pisses Ethan off, since our shower turned into shower sex and left him with no hot water. We go grab a coffee at the small coffee shop across the street before she heads home. According to Ana, the best way to start the day is with coffee and orgasms. Something I made sure to make note of, and would be sure to deliver on again and again!

It's been a week since the first time I felt myself inside her, and we have spent time every single one of those 7 days tangled between sheets, wet in the shower, or parked in the Jeep in the back of the bar parking lot. Ana and I have defiled every surface we can imagine.

When I got home from work, the giant box I'd been expecting was waiting for me outside of the front door. Ethan helped me carry it to my room, where I spent the next hour setting up the space by the balcony with meticulous care. It's going to be a place just for Ana. When I set my mind to something, it's happening, and it's going to be fucking amazing, it has to be, that's just who

I am. I spread out the blankets to create a soft, inviting feel. I arrange the pillows in a comforting mess, making sure there's a variety of shapes and sizes for leaning or lounging. It looks pretty damn close to the Insta photo I used for inspiration.

I step back and take in the finished corner, feeling a rush of satisfaction. It's a small, personal space dedicated just for her, a spot where she can unwind and enjoy some downtime. I imagine her curled up in the blankets, hopefully with me, but also utilizing it as she voiced she would, curled up with a good book on a rainy day.

The anticipation of having her here this weekend makes me grin. I'm excited for her to see what I've done, to know she has a special place just for her in my home. I can't wait for her to arrive. It's a small gesture I know, but it's my way of showing her how much I care, how much I appreciate the time we spend together and how much I enjoy having her here.

Her apartment building is getting all new hardwood, and they will be staining and sealing her floors on Friday night. I took it as the perfect opportunity to spend time together. She has to wait at least 24 hours before going back to her apartment to ensure the fumes settle, so I was able to convince her to just stay the entire weekend at my place. Ethan will be staying with his parents to help them with all of the finishing touches for their annual Halloween party. That shit is unreal. It takes them weeks to decorate.

The idea of Ethan being away causes my imagination to run wild with thoughts of my weekend alone with my girl. My Stitch.

The image of us curled in this dark cozy corner, only the string lights and small lamp illuminating the room, makes me hope there is some sort of set back with her floors.

Maybe they won't cure correctly and they'll have to redo them.

I can picture the lights dancing off her bright blue eyes and how they will sparkle. I can imagine the way her lips will glisten as she smiles. Fuck. Her eyes and perfect fucking lips are my Achilles heel. I just want more of them. I can't wait to get lost in her as she reads, curled up in my lap- preferably naked, so I can make good on starting the mornings the only way she prefers, with coffee and orgasms.

Ana

"**K**NOX?" I YELL FROM the open front door.

"Hey, Stitch," he yells from the bedroom. "I'm in my room. Do you mind closing the door? I just carried a package in, and you came before I could go back to close it."

"Sure thing. Hey, I stopped and picked up some pizza. I hope you're hungry."

"Starving! Can you come help me real quick, before we eat?"

I grab us both a slice, place them on a napkin and head to his room. I just about drop both slices when I walk in, stunned at what I see.

"Knox, this is incredible. Is this for me?"

"Well, I'm not the cozy corner type, and I don't see any other hot chicks staying here."

"I'm only here for two days," I quip.

"You mentioned how amazing it would be," he lowers his voice to a seductive whisper. "And, I don't care if you're here for two seconds, I would do anything to make that smile of yours stick around, plus it ups my chances of you putting out," he teases.

I set the pizza on his dresser and rush to him. I kiss him hard, our lips pressing together with a fervor leaving me breathless. The intensity of the moment is palpable, a mix of urgency and desire making my heart race. As I pull away, I let my fingers trail lightly down his chest, savoring the warmth of his skin, damp from sweat beneath my touch.

He must have just finished this.

Knox standing before me is another sight that stuns me as I take it in. I have seen him naked, yet the sight never truly sunk in. I'm taken off guard again by his hard muscles, as he stands in front of me shirtless and clearly sweaty from the hard work he put into this space. In contrast to my soft exterior, Knox is firm, rippled, and pure sex standing in front me.

Without a word, I make my way over to the dark, cozy corner of the room. It perfectly complements the moody vibe that is Knox Reed. It's a quiet retreat, tucked away from the rest of the space, and it feels like a secret haven all its own. The corner is framed by the balcony door, which allows just enough light to filter through, casting a soft, muted glow over the area.

The centerpiece of this cozy nook is a black papasan chair, its cushion a deep, dark gray, seeming almost black in the dim light. The chair's rounded shape invites you to sink into it, and the olive throw draped over it enhances the feeling of warmth and comfort. The throw is so dark, it blends seamlessly with the chair, adding to the intimate and snug atmosphere.

Next to the chair, sits a small round table looking almost like it was plucked right from a charming café. The table holds a lamp with a soft, warm light casting a gentle glow over the space, and a vase filled with fresh flowers. The flowers add a touch of color and life, their subtle fragrance mingling with the cozy, musky scent of the room.

How the hell did he do this?

On the table next to the lamp, there's a dark green coffee mug matching the color of the blanket draped over the chair perfectly. Only the mug is inscribed with the message: "Busier than a cucumber in a women's prison." It's a playful touch, adding a bit of Knox's playful personality to the corner.

"What is this?" Laughing out loud, as I pick it up, "Where the hell do you find shit like this?"

"Amazon, where do you shop?"

"My Amazon and your Amazon look very different," I joke.

"It's not a fucking 'for you' page, Stitch, Amazon has what you are looking for. I was looking for a funny inappropriate mug."

We sit together on the papasan chair, the world outside the balcony door distant and irrelevant. Admiring the decorations I put up last week, I'm curled into Knox's lap, feeling the steady rise and fall of his chest beneath me. The chair around us is a soft, round embrace, creating a cozy cocoon that feels like it was made just for us.

In one hand, I hold the last piece of pizza, savoring each bite. The cheesy, gooey slice is warm and satisfying. The pizza box, now empty, rests between us, its once-crisp cardboard now slightly greasy.

As I finish the last bite and set the crust aside, Knox slides the pizza box onto the floor with a casual motion. The box lands with a soft thud. His hands, now free, curl around me with a gentle possessiveness, pulling me closer into his hard body.

His arms wrap around me like a warm blanket, his touch both grounding and soothing. I nestle deeper into his lap, feeling his body radiate warmth against mine. His fingers lightly trace patterns on my arm.

We sit in comfortable silence, the only sounds are the gentle rustling of the throw blanket and the occasional creak of the papasan chair as we shift slightly. Outside, the city lights twinkle in the evening, casting a soft glow through the balcony door.

The moment is serene and intimate. Knox's presence is strong, overwhelming my senses. I lean my head back against his chest, and breathe him in.

The room feels warm, suspended in time. Everything feels just right, and I have never felt more welcome, more comfortable, and more protected than I do at this moment.

"I'm glad you like it," he says.

"I love it."

My response is followed by a slow sensual kiss, just after I lick a bit of pizza sauce off the lip ring on his lower lip.

"What made you get this?" I ask, brushing my finger across the ring circling his bottom lip. "I thought college athletes couldn't have piercings."

He inhales slightly, "I decided if I can't do what I've always been passionate about, I should do something I've always wanted to do but never could."

"I love that, Knox. You were able to put a positive spin on a terrible situation."

"Trust me, it sounds optimistic, Stitch, but I was really broken inside before I met you."

"I'm not sure I did anything truly significant." I smile.

"You are everything," he replies as he brushes his knuckle across my bottom lip. On a deep exhale he looks at me, his voice heavy with memories. "That night we met, I had Oxy in my pocket. I'd gone to see the doctor a few days before, and was feeling so overwhelmed and desperate to escape my own misery. But then I saw you, and everything faded away. You gave me the relief I was seeking, because for the first time in a long time, I felt hope. I wanted to know you, and getting to know you has pulled me out of that dark place."

My eyes widen, I'm speechless. I reach out and touch his hand, trying to steady my voice. "I'm glad you changed my mind," I finally say with a chuckle not wanting to make the moment too heavy.

"What exactly have you changed your mind about?" he teases.

"Spending time with you." I smile. "Knox. I've never spent a significant amount of time with someone else romantically. My dad ruined the idea of romance for me, so I appreciate you allowing me the space to navigate this without the pressure of putting a label on it, creating space for us to see where this goes naturally."

"I look forward to spending time with you, Stitch. I needed something to look forward to. No bullshit, remember?" He smiles looking deep into my eyes.

Without a word, he slowly kisses down my neck and over my collarbone. Trailing small nips down my body as he undresses me. He stands us both up and then kneels in front of me. He slides his hands up my torso and then back down, slipping his thumbs in the waistband of my sweats and pulls them down, taking my lace panties with them. "Fuck baby! Your pussy is so goddamn perfect." He rolls his teeth over his lip ring, and I clench my thighs to dull the ache growing between my legs, feeling my arousal pooling. He goes back to trailing light kisses over my body, only this time he starts much lower, moving down my legs and then slowly back up.

Nip.

Nip.

Just as he reaches the place I need him most, he brushes the tip of his nose across my opening, and then he stands up gliding his hands on top of my t-shirt over the swell of my breasts, and then back down.

Nip.

Nip.

"This thing is staying on," he growls as he lays my t-shirt back over my hips. "It's my fucking favorite. Go to the bed and get on your hands and knees, Ana. I want to see that plump ass peeking out from underneath that fuuucking shirt," he draws out the words with lust painting his voice.

Without question I do as I am told, peeking over my shoulder as I hear his pants hit the floor. I hold my gaze, unwavering resolve as I listen to his demands.

"Put a pillow under your hips, and lay your tits against the mattress," he demands. "I want to see each curve as I fuck you."

My usual self-assured demeanor softens into a deep, accommodating presence, willing to follow his lead and fulfill his desires with a quiet unspoken submission.

Even though Knox has not played baseball in almost a year, his body is still one of a collegiate athlete. He is tall and lean with broad shoulders curving with each muscle spilling over onto his back. His pecs are chiseled and square, and each ripple in his abs shows off just how much time he spends working on his body. My eyes trace the muscles down his torso as they slip into a tight v just above the swell of his cock. Hard. Swollen. A small bead of precum gathering at the tip. I lick my lips wanting a taste. Just as I move my mouth in the direction of his cock, Knox smacks my ass so hard I gasp.

"This ass is mine, Anabelle," he shudders menacingly. "And I'm enjoying the view, you fucking stay right there." He then slowly rubs his hand over the red skin, soothing the burn and then brushes his lips across it with sweet kisses. This version of Knox is my favorite. Hot and cold. Sweet yet domineering. Being intimate with Knox is like sailing stormy seas; calm one moment and violently possessed by waves the next.

He bends down running his tongue along my entrance. Starting against the cool metal of my piercing, trailing the length of my opening and then circling the small hole between my cheeks. I clinch, surprising myself, thrilled by the sensation.

"Mmmm," I mutter.

"You like that? You want more?"

"I don't know," I whisper honestly. It's something I've never done before.

"What *do* you know, Ana?"

"I know I want you inside me," I reply with bated breath.

Just then, he slams inside me without warning. As much as Knox loves being in control, he is always quick to fulfill every one of my requests. While the motion is slow, it is hard and forceful. A loud gasp leaves my mouth.

He never lets up. He never stops moving. He moves his hips back and forth, changing the pace with small circles, reaching places I didn't know existed. Just when I am about to fall over the edge he grabs my hips, and flips me over.

"There's my girl." His tone becomes tender and full of emotion. "There is just something about this position, standing the test of time. It must be the view." He smiles, placing a soft kiss on my lips.

He slides himself back into me, but his pace slows, and his thrusts deepen. We make love.

We make love!

Today, March 1

"Tidal waves, they rip right through me"
-Blink 182

Ana

I'M COLD.

I can't move.

Knox is here.

He's been here.

I love him, I love him so much, so much the time we lost is painful. So much has changed between us, so much has changed us… but he's still here.

My love for Knox Reed is deep, complex, and hard to describe.

I hear soft footsteps, and then a voice calling out, they sound as if they are playing on a video. It's him,

Riker.

My love for him is unwavering.

Direct.

It's a powerful force that drives me. I'm not afraid of this love, there is no hesitation, no doubt. When it comes to Riker, my love is clear, concise.

So easy to articulate.

Halloween, Three Years Ago

"Fate fell short this time"
-Blink 182

Knox

ANA'S APARTMENT floors were done on schedule, and she went back home on Sunday night. I miss her in my bed. It's now Saturday, and even though it's been almost a week, my pillows still smell like her shampoo which seems to help dull the ache of her not being here.

Ethan's parents are having their Halloween party tonight. I asked Ana if she wanted to come with me, but she and Blake had plans of their own to go out with Blake's best friend from high school.

So, here I am by myself, beer in hand with thoughts of Ana moaning my name, as the hot water trailed down her back when I took her from behind in the shower at her apartment this morning.

When I woke up, I rolled over to grab my phone from where I left it after we FaceTimed last night, and the faint smell of her shampoo on my pillow made my dick instantly hard. I laid there with my hand lazily stroking my cock for a few minutes before I decided there was no substitution for the real thing. I quickly showered, threw on some clothes, and picked up coffee to surprise her.

When I showed up unexpectedly we lost control. Our coffee got cold, but shit, she was so fucking hot and needy when I slid inside her.

The sound of my name being called over the music, snaps me back to the present moment in the garage at the party. Ethan's parents decorate like they are putting on a haunted house for paid entry. All of the walls are lined with plastic mimicking a brick wall, covered in cobwebs. There are life size figurines spread through the entire house, each room with a distinct theme. The garage, where we landed once we made our rounds, is littered with clowns, cobwebs, and strobe lights, making it hard for me to make out who was calling my name.

"Knox," I hear again as a hand shoots up in the air. An arm attached to a slender blond Barbie in a tight pink dress and matching shiny pink heels.

April. Fuck.

"Hey, April. What are you doing here? I didn't know you and Ethan knew each other?"

How in the hell does Ethan know April?

Why didn't he tell me she would be here?

"Who's Ethan?" she questioned. I bent down and gave her a hug and kiss on the cheek. April is a sweet girl. A little needy and clingy, sometimes a bit overbearing, but she kept me company during some of my hardest months, so I have no reason to shrug her off even though I have no intention of taking her home tonight.

"My roommate, this is his parents' party. They moved in here a few years ago," I answered.

"Weird! We've never met, but I love his mom! I thought you lived at home?" she asks. "Anyways there is someone…" April's words fade out as I spot a short brunette in a skin tight black one piece with skeleton bones painted on the front and back. Her hair pulled up into a half ponytail, the rest cascading down her back in loose curls, and red converse on her feet. Her face is not painted, it is all very understated, but making quite the statement to me from across the room.

"Excuse me," I say to April. Placing my hand on her shoulder to move past her.

Ana is standing at the keg with the same tall redhead she was with at the bar who is dressed as Poison Ivy, the perfect costume for her vibrant red hair. Even though Ana and I have spent a lot of time together, our time together has never lined up with her roommate's schedule. "You must be Blake," I say as I lean around Ana whose back is to me, put my hand out to shake her friend's hand just as I kiss her cheek.

Turning with a little jump she says, "Knox? Oh my god, what are you doing here?"

"This is Ethan's parents' party. What are you doing here?"

"Blake's best friend from high school grew up down the street. She's a little obnoxious if you ask me," Ana whispers in my ear. "Her name is April, you can't miss her, she's dressed as Barbie." My stomach turns.

"Knox, this is who I wanted you to meet," April says pointing to the redhead as she approaches us from where I left her. "Blake and I have been friends since our sophomore year in high school. She moved about 45 minutes from here after college, so we don't see each other very often anymore." She stops talking just long enough to see my fingers interlaced with Ana's. She looks down at our hands, and slowly roams her eyes over Ana's entire body as she finally asks, "How do you two know each other?"

Ana doesn't hesitate in her response, "Knox and I met at the bar I work at a few weeks ago, and we've been hanging out since."

"Oh good," April interjected. "The way he's holding your hand I thought it might be more serious, and that would be really *awkward*," April drew out with a sigh.

"Let's go get a drink, Stitch," I say, pulling Ana towards the door leading into the house, wanting nothing more than a quick escape.

"Did you sleep with her?" Ana asks as we make our way into the next room.

"Yes," I huff. "A few times. We've only known each other for like two months. I needed some mindless release with everything going on with my arm. Trust me, she is not my type. You have nothing to worry about." I'm rambling. Ana places her hand on my chest in a soothing way.

"Ok," she replies without question and starts walking again. Her confidence is so sexy.

Throughout the night, Ana and I had our moments of being a little reckless, sneaking away from the group to make out, leaving us both breathless. Each stolen moment was filled with heat and intensity, our hands exploring and lingering in places hinting at what was to come later, making my dick hard as hell. Even when we weren't alone, we would steal glances at each other across the room, our eyes communicating more than words ever could. There was something thrilling about our unspoken connection, about knowing we had this special thing between us, even amidst the chaos of a party.

I loved that we could be together and not have to be right next to each other all night. We could enjoy the night and our time apart while still feeling the pull of each other across the room. It was a balance of intimacy and independence that felt just right.

The room was a swirl of colors and sounds, the music thumping in the background as laughter and conversation mingled in the air. Despite the buzz of activity around us, there was always this quiet undercurrent of heat between Ana and me, a thread pulling us together no matter how far apart we drifted during the night.

When we did come back together, it was fucking hot, our smiles and touches, a promise. The playful glances, the stolen kisses, and the shared laughter made the night unforgettable, a perfect blend of fun and intimacy only making me want her that much more.

We spent the next few hours laughing, drinking, and taking shots. The energy of the night was electric, fueled by good company and the kind of carefree spirit that comes with a few too many drinks.

Now, she's waiting in line to use the bathroom, and when it's her turn, I decide to follow her in. She spins around as I quickly close the door behind me. I take her phone out of her hands, set it on the counter, push her up against the wall and find myself buried in her neck, one of my favorite places to be.

"Your hair smells amazing, Stitch," I say, breathing her in. "What is it?"

"Lavender," she replies with a soft moan.

"Lavender… I think I fucking love lavender," I whisper as I place a slow kiss on her collarbone. My hands start roaming her body, stopping at the nape of her neck as I slowly snake one hand around her throat and then kiss her. She gets so wet when I do this.

"Knox, I really don't want to get all hot and heavy in a bathroom," she interrupts, pushing me off her. "It's gross. Plus, it's hard to focus on you with a giant ass werewolf growling in my face," she laughs.

There was not a single inch of the house undecorated. Including the shitter. All of the lights in the bathroom had been replaced with purple ones, stickers littered the walls and the mirror above the sink was covered in "bloody" handprints. Even the shower was decorated. The walls were draped in fake vines resembling thick foliage covering each corner and edge. Plastic trees and branches were strategically placed with lights flashing through the leaves creating a haunted scene. It was incredible, actually.

"Tonight?" I ask.

"Not tonight, I have a meeting tomorrow, and I'm beat," she says as she shoves me out so she can pee.

I sigh in disappointment, and give the wolf one more look as I think to myself, *I wonder where they keep all this shit?*

After a few rounds of flip cup and beer pong, and a couple more shots, Blake and Ana get ready to leave. I walk with them out front, Ana and I kiss goodnight, our bodies gravitating to one another like we both need the friction. "I'll go home with you," I say, repeating my offer from earlier.

"No you will not, Knox. I have to work tomorrow, and neither one of us slept much last night between the naughty late night FaceTime and sexcapades this morning. Plus my vag is a little sore from the assault you gave it," she laughs.

"You liked it."

"Doesn't mean it doesn't need a night off," she counters as she kisses me and then ducks into the Uber Blake ordered.

I stand in the driveway watching until the car pulls away and then make my way back inside, grab a drink, and head back to the bathroom to take a leak.

"Knox," April says just as I start to piss, pushing her way in through the door I clearly forgot to lock, and then closing and locking it quickly.

"What the fuck April, get out of here," I say.

"What?" she teases, pulling her top down, her large tits with perfectly round pink nipples staring at me. Nipples I would usually be eager to wrap my mouth around.

"April, stop it, ok. I'm going to finish my piss and then I'm going to get drunk, *without you,*" I emphasize for good measure.

"Well since you have it out," she says, trying to reach over and grab my dick, just as I turn and zip quickly.

"April!" I shout with a little chuckle, trying not to be too big of an asshole. "Listen, Ana and I are not official, but I really like her, so this," I say, pointing between us, "this is done."

I continue to fasten my pants as I open the door deciding to get the fuck out of here, quickly. I take one step and bump right into Ana, hurt fills her eyes as she locks them with mine, she immediately turns and walks towards the door.

Fuck.

Ana

"**W**AIT," I SAY JUST as we hit the highway. "I'm sorry, I think I left my phone in the bathroom back at the party."

"That's what happens when you're dick drunk," Blake replies. "Can we go back really quick?" she asks the driver.

"For an extra $10 tip."

"Deal," I agree.

It took us about 5 minutes to get back from the highway, and I didn't want to waste any more of the driver's time, so I decided to sneak in quickly, grab my phone, and sneak back out before Knox saw me. I knew if he did, we would have another 15-minute goodbye with both of us left hot and panting.

When I get inside the bathroom door is closed, so I wait. "April," I hear a muffled voice chuckle from inside.

This chick sure gets around.

A few seconds later the door flies open and Knox comes barreling into me, fumbling with his pants, April hot on his heels… pulling her boobs back into her dress.

The sudden burst of activity leaves me momentarily stunned, my eyes darting between Knox and April, trying to process the scene unfolding in front of me. Knox's expression is one I've never seen, maybe a mix of embarrassment and regret, while April's flustered look suggests a hurried end to whatever had just fucking happened in there. Knox's eyes meet mine for a split second, before he tries to regain his composure, mouth open but nothing coming out. April is still standing behind him adjusting her dress with a sigh, her cheeks looking flushed.

What the actual fuck?

Without a second thought, I turn and rage-walk towards the front door. My steps are heavy and purposeful, each one echoing my frustration and confusion. I'm seething, my mind a whirlwind of emotions.

My heart pounds as I try to reign in my emotions. I need to clear my head, to figure out what the hell I just walked in on, and what I do next. I take a deep breath, trying to calm down.

I take my first step out the front door when I hear, "Ana, wait!" Knox shouts. "Anabelle, please wait."

I spin around, Knox stumbling as I stop him in his path. "Don't you dare fucking call me Anabelle ever again, Knox. I only allow people close to me to use my full name, and you just lost that fucking privilege when I walked in to find you in the bathroom balls deep in some whore."

"Ana, do you really think I was balls deep in there?"

"Knox I may not have seen you screwing her, but I know what I saw when you two were leaving the bathroom."

Shit! My phone.

I push past him and charge back into the house.

"Ana, where are you going?" he asks, chasing me in the direction we had just come.

"I left my phone in the bathroom when you had your tongue down my throat and your hands around my neck, but guess I'm not the only one who fell for your bullshit tonight."

I'm back to the bathroom in seconds and thankfully it's open. I grab my phone, feeling it's reassuring weight in my hand as I turn back to head to the front door. The anger still simmers within me, driving my steps with a fierce intensity. As I move past a small crowd of people gathered by the shot room, their curious glances and murmured conversations slowly blend into background noise.

The vibrant sounds of the party, the laughter, the clinking of glasses, the thumping bass of the music, are a stark contrast to the hurricane brewing inside me. I push through the crowd, not bothering to offer any excuses or apologies for my abrupt departure. My only focus is to get out, to put some distance between myself and the chaotic scene inside.

Reaching the front door, I yank it open with more force than necessary. The cool night air rushes in, offering a brief respite from the stifling atmosphere inside. I step out onto the porch, the wooden planks rock beneath my feet. The streetlight casts a halo of light around me, but I barely notice the details of the scene. My mind is still focused on the swirling shit show of emotions inside me and the immediate need to reach out for some kind of support.

"Ana, please, I wa, " Knox is right behind me again.

"Knox, please just shut the fuck up," I interrupt him mid sentence and make my way back to the Uber, Knox follows close behind me. "We are not together, Konx. There is no label on us," I say pointing between us. "But I told you I don't like bullshit, and I was not into your fuckboy persona. So pardon me while I see my way out of this little game you have going on here. I'm just not into it!" I climb back into the Uber and slam the door before he has the chance to say anything else.

A wave of nausea hits me. My stomach churns with a wave of jealousy, heartbreak, and regret.

I should have just let him come home with me and this would have never happened. No! Fuck that! If this is who he really is, this was bound to happen eventually! No time like the present to see his true colors. Only they don't feel like his true colors. This doesn't seem like the Knox I know. Maybe he's not really the Knox I think I know, maybe it's a front. No, that can't be true! I'm so confused, the reality of what I saw tonight and the person I have spent so much time with leaving me feeling stranded in the eye of the storm.

Shit! I feel like the ground beneath me has given way, leaving me unsteady and overwhelmed by this sea of emotions. Every detail of Knox emerging from the bathroom burned into my mind. A lump is forming in my throat, and my vision blurry from unshed tears building as we pull away from the house.

"Ana, What happened?" Blake urges as I slide back into the Uber.

"I don't want to talk about it." Tears silently streaming down my face.

"Ana, what did he do? I swear, I will fucking kill him if he hurt you," she says, offering blind and unwavering support.

Instead of answering, I just stare out the window, silent.

Knox Reed fading into the night behind us.

Today, March 1

"Pick me up now, I need you so bad"
-Blink 182

Knox

"PLEASE BE OK, PLEASE fucking be ok!" I whisper to myself on repeat as I pace the waiting room. My thoughts are moving faster than I can process them.

How could I let this happen? My instincts as an athlete are so much better than this. I saw the motherfucker coming, I knew he was headed towards us. She was on the inside, I thought he'd hit me instead. I should have pushed her away. NEVER, in my wildest fucking dreams would I have thought she'd move towards me, towards the danger. I should have pushed her out of the motherfucking way.

How the fuck did I let this happen?

Winter, Two And A Half Years Ago

"Have you hurt like this before?
When your heart's already torn
When your tears are on my mind
We fall apart there every time"
-Blink 182

Knox

IT'S BEEN THREE MONTHS. THREE FUCKING MONTHS. That's how long it's been since Ana ran out of the party, since I've heard her voice or seen her face. I've gone through hell, each day a different loop on the worst rollercoaster ride. There have been days where I feel optimistic, days I am so pissed I can't stand it, and days I don't give a shit and want to just forget her completely and move on.

I've called, left messages, and sent texts, one after another, each more desperate than the last. I even sent flowers to her house, hoping they might bridge the space that's grown between us, make her talk to me, but I should have known better, that's not her. She's not going to engage in any bullshit.

I've replayed that night over and over in my head for what feels like the millionth time, the scene of her running out, her face a mixture of hurt and anger, the memory haunts me to this day. I don't understand how it all went so wrong. Everything was fine before that, how the fuck did I let this happen?

Every message I've sent feels like a shot in the dark, every call an attempt to claw my way back into her life. But nothing has worked. The silence in return is deafening, and more painful than any words she could have said.

I've tried to move on, to distract myself with work, with friends, with anything that might fill the void she left behind. But the emptiness remains, a constant reminder of what I lost. The nights are the hardest, lying awake in bed, staring at the ceiling, my mind full of regret and what-ifs. To make matters worse, I'm only six weeks post op from my second surgery, and have been limited in activity by the hinge brace adorning my arm, only getting to return to work this week on "light duty". The pain this time around was naturally just more intense. Between the fact they were fucking around with previously damaged tissue and the tylenol and ibuprofen regimen I'm on to avoid opioids, this has been so much harder. Drugs that don't pack a punch, don't do jack shit for pain in comparison to the hard stuff. Given my lack of activity, pain induced frustration, and lack of sex, I have not had much to distract me from the constant thoughts of her.

I don't know where she is or what she's doing. I don't even know if she's still angry with me or if she's moved on entirely. I'm left with nothing but the fragments of what we were, leaving nothing but a motherfucking shattered mess.

I wish I could turn back time, fix what went wrong, and show her how much she means to me. But I'm stuck in this limbo, waiting for a sign, a chance, anything that might bring her back into my life.

She is a master avoider, evading the entire situation. She is hiding in the shadows waiting for me to give up. Jokes on her, that is not fucking happening. I love her, and I know she loves me too.

The last time I went to the bar, about a month ago hoping to run into her, she wasn't there. I decided today I'm gonna give it another go.

I walk into the empty bar and immediately spot Blake. "Hey, is Ana working today?" I ask. It's about an hour before they open, and I figured it was my best shot at talking to her if she was here.

"She quit, Knox. Her last day was almost a week ago." She had an expression etched on her face I couldn't read, but from what I can gather, she's struggling to find a way to navigate this conversation.

I just stare at Blake, blankly. I don't really know what to say. Ana always said this job was temporary. She has a marketing degree, but was waiting for the right job to come along to start using it. She wanted to do something fun with it, not just work a mundane job every day.

"She got a job with a hotel in town, and will be doing all of their marketing from home," Blake explains.

"That doesn't make sense, she was waiting for something different, something exciting to work on. She was always looking at marketing jobs with different resort travel companies, amusement parks, not small hotels in town," I argue.

"Knox, she has a lot going on, she was a little desperate, and it's just not a good time right now."

"Desperate?" I question. "What's going on, Blake?" I don't wait for her to respond, my frustration clearly taking over. "Listen, can you just please, talk to her, get her to call me? I need to explain what happened. The thought that she believes I slept with April, or even fooled around with her is making me fucking sick. It's been five months, and I just, I have to talk to her ok? Please, Blake," I beg.

"She knows," she pauses, her words hitting me with the force of a sledgehammer to the chest. "She knows the truth, Knox. April came by, her and I were talking and I told her how upset you have both been, and she felt bad. She saw Ana leave that night and I guess after some time passed, her conscience got the best of her. She came by and told Ana everything. She thought you two were just hooking up, casual like you were with her, so she let it go that night and never said anything. After we talked, she felt really bad, so she told her everything, Knox. But…" She pauses for a few seconds, clearly thinking through her next words. "By the time April came by, Ana had some shit come up. Listen, it's not my shit to tell, but she will talk to you when she's ready. She's just not in a good place right now. It's not a good time. She needs space, so just give it to her. That's the best thing you can do," Blake says as she continues cleaning the bar getting it ready to open.

She knew and she was still avoiding me.

What happened? What made her need time?

"Can you at least tell her I'm trying?" I all but beg.

"Sure, Knox," she sighs.

With a heavy heart and a mind full of frustration I leave the bar racking my brain. I'm worse off now than I was before my conversation with Blake. Deciding I need a distraction, I pick up the phone to call Ethan. It only rings a few times before he answers. "She fucking quit her job dude," I say immediately.

"That's weird. What is she doing?" he asks.

"Apparently she's working from home for some hotel doing their marketing or some shit."

"That's cool," Ethan replies, "That's what she's been wanting, right?"

"Not exactly." I take a long breath. "I need a distraction from all this shit! Wanna go out tonight?"

"Yeah, I'll be home at 6."

"Thanks man." I hang up the phone wondering what the actual fuck is going on with her, but clearly she doesn't want me to know.

After talking myself into listening to Blake, the only conclusion I can make is if I love Ana, and I do, I need to give her the time she needs. I haven't made any attempts to contact her in the last week since going to the bar, and it's killing me. I think missing her is making me love her even more.

My love for her is the only thing keeping me going, and the only thing racing through my mind on my way home from work. Suddenly a craving hits me, tacos from my favorite spot.

Well this is a nice change of pace, craving something other than Ana.

It's a little bit out of the way, about fifteen minutes from home, but worth every second of the drive. The place is known for its street tacos, they are pretty fucking legendary.

The corn tortillas are always grilled to perfection, warm with a crisp edge adding just the right texture. The carne asada is the star of the show: tender, juicy, and packed with flavor bursting in every bite. It's the kind of meal that sticks with you.

I always meant to bring Ana here. I imagined her sitting across from me, savoring the tacos, maybe even laughing at my overly enthusiastic descriptions of the place. She'd love it so much she'd moan as she stuffed her face, and the sight would make me crave a different taco completely.

But now, as I drive through the quiet streets, the empty passenger seat beside me feels like a stark reminder of what's missing. I can almost hear her laughter, see her smile as she enjoys the food. The anticipation of sharing this experience with her was something I looked forward to, and now, it's a bittersweet thought.

I pull into the parking lot, the smell of tacos filling the air immediately making my stomach growl. I turn off the Jeep, and pull my sunglasses off the visor. The sun is bright as shit reflecting off the wet ground.

I catalog every following motion in vivid detail, because it's when my heart broke into a million fucking pieces.

I watch as Ana walks out the restaurant door, bundled in a jacket, boots, and a beanie, carrying a to-go bag looking heavy against her small frame. The cold air whips around her making her hair dance wildly. She is right there. My breath catches in my throat when I see the guy she's walking towards, his phone in his hand. I look him up and down, his light brown hair blowing in the wind. He is slightly shorter than me, but his presence feels threatening the minute I see the warm smile break across his face when he sees Ana. With effortless familiarity, he walks up to her, gently taking the bag from her hands. He walks her to the car, a beat-up sedan and it somehow feels more welcoming than anything I can offer. As he opens the door and tucks her inside, a simple act, it feels like a knife twisting in my heart. It is such a simple action, one he handles with practiced ease, as if it is woven into the fabric of their daily life.

I sit here, rooted to the seat in my Jeep, as the reality of the scene crashes over me. Each moment is a brutal reminder of the distance lying between us. The way she seems to have moved on and is completely over me. The way he cares for her is enough to make my world feel like it is completely breaking apart. The sight of them together, the easy companionship they share is a stark contrast to the chaos and confusion swirling inside me. It was such a simple act, but it shatters me.

She's seeing someone?

I exit the Jeep, stopping just in front of the sedan Ana had climbed into. My gaze deliberate, holding steady to draw her attention. I want her to see just how pissed and broken I am, and let her sit with that image in her mind for the rest of the fucking night. My eye contact is clear, creating a brief uncomfortable connection. My stomach hurls. My heart crushes.

She looks up and as we make eye contact, I can see the hurt and shock written all over her face. It's as if she is caught in a whirlwind of regret, but maybe that's just my wishful thinking. For a brief moment her gaze holds mine, and I swear I can see a silent apology words could never convey. It's as if she is pleading for me to understand, even though she knows it's not possible. I turn and walk inside to order food I no longer have an appetite for, and the sedan pulls away, with my Ana inside.

My 15 minute drive home is long and silent. Full of conflicting emotions. The heater blowing in my face fights against the winter chill, but the cold emptiness inside me is impossible to shake. My hands grip the wheel, knuckles white with tension. Each turn of the wheel feels mechanical, like I'm on autopilot.

Street after street, I keep drifting back to the moment she walked out, the way he gently took the bag from her, the way she slid into his car, those simple acts scarred my heart. I can't forget her gaze when she saw me.

As I drive, the trees around me are bare and lacking life, a faint outline of lights and shadows. The drive feels endless, stretching out in painful moments that go on forever. I sit in the car in the lot outside my building, dreading the next steps I have to take. The warmth of my apartment feels muted, overshadowed by the weight of what I'd seen. With a heavy sigh, I turn off the engine, brace myself for a difficult night, and walk inside.

Now I'm sitting in the dark of my apartment with my tacos open on the table, downing beer after beer and completely ignoring the food in front of me. Just then I hear a soft knock at the door. When I open it, standing there is my girl. Only she's not my girl. She's someone else's girl.

"Hi," she offers softly.

"Hi? Hi… What the fuck Ana? Why are you here?"

"I've been avoiding you," she says flatly. "I… there is something I've been needing to tell you, but I don't really have the words, I um…"

She pauses for what feels like forever.

"You what, Ana? You walked in on me zipping my pants up because I was trying to piss and April thought she had an opportunity while my pants were down? Didn't care to let me explain what actually happened, and then avoided me for FUCKING MONTHS even after April told you the fucking truth?" I shout. My hands have clenched into fists at my side.

"No, Knox… Well technically yes, but no, I, "

"You what?" I cut in, "You fucked another guy, and now you're getting tacos with him and coming here to tell me what, Ana? That you're in love with him?"

Tears start falling down her face.

She is crying.

She keeps trying to interrupt me, but I don't let her.

"Knox," it is soft, coming off her lips, covered in tears and heartbreak.

Her cry quickly transforms into full-blown sobs, each one wracking her body with uncontrollable waves of anguish. Her shoulders shake violently, and her breath comes in sharp, desperate gasps. Tears continue to stream down her cheeks, carving clean paths through the streaks of makeup, and leaving glistening trails on her skin.

Ana clutches her stomach with both hands, as though trying to hold herself together, her fingers digging into her sides as if to keep everything from spilling out. Her whole body trembles with the intensity of her sobs, and her eyes, red and swollen, reflect a pain so raw and palpable it feels like it's reaching out to engulf me too. The sight of her struggling so visibly sends a knife of regret and sadness through my chest.

But I can't hear it. I don't want to know what the words sound like coming off her lips.

"Ana, seeing you with someone else was a motherfucking punch in the gut. You have been avoiding me over a fucking misunderstanding, it's like a slap in the face. You discarded me. You assumed the worst of me. Threw me out like trash. Then I see you all cozy with someone else. Fuck that. It's funny, you claim you don't like bullshit, don't play games, but that is exactly what you're doing. You moved on, so I guess it's time for me to do the same."

I slam the door in her face with a force that echoes through the empty hallway. The sound of the door's finality splinters in my ears, a harsh punctuation to the chaos that just unfolded. The weight of the decision settles heavily on my shoulders, and I hear her footsteps moving down the hall, her sobs fading into the distance.

The cold silence that follows is unbearable. My breath comes out in ragged gasps as I sink to the floor. Everything feels like it's falling apart. My mind is a whirlwind of regret, confusion, and self-loathing. I try to pull myself together, but it's no use. I'm drowning in the fucking aftermath of my own making.

I stumble to the kitchen, awestruck by what just happened and driven by a need to numb this pain. A bottle of whiskey becomes my escape. Ignoring the painful truth that this could be my undoing, I pour a heavy glass, the amber liquid sloshing around as if it holds the solutions to my problems and the answers to all my questions.

The alcohol burns its way down, and for a moment, it blots out the sharp edges of my emotions. I take another drink, then another, desperate for the numbness to come. The room tilts and spins around me as the liquor takes effect, my vision blurring with each swallow.

I collapse onto the couch, clutching the bottle as if it's the only thing keeping me tethered to reality. My head is a rush of memories and lost chances, and every attempt to piece it together only makes the chaos worse. The darkness wraps around me, suffocating me.

How the fuck did we get here?

Ana

"BLAKE, I DON'T KNOW what to do." The words escape my lips, drowned in uncontrollable sobs as I bury my face into her shoulder. We're curled up on the couch in our living room, the place that used to feel like a sanctuary but now feels stifling, as if the walls are closing in.

"I have never seen him so upset," I continue, my voice trembling with fear and regret.

Blake sighs, her tone dripping with both sympathy and brutal honesty. "Well, I hate to tell you this, but he's kind of right, Ana."

What she says cuts deep, but I know she isn't trying to hurt me, she's just being real. "You assumed the worst of him. You knew how he felt about you, yet you still believed he betrayed you. I can see why he's hurt."

Her words hang in the air, like the truth I've been avoiding.

"But…" She pauses, taking a moment to choose her next words carefully. "I also completely understand why you believed it. It looked so bad, Ana. You had every right to feel upset and to think he hooked up with her. This is a shitty situation, but ignoring it isn't going to make it any better."

I feel my heart drop further. I want to argue, to explain my reaction was just a defense mechanism, a way to protect myself from more pain. But deep down, I know she's right. I let my fears and what I believed I saw drive a wedge between us, and now I'm paying the price.

"Blake, I can't go back there," I finally say, my voice barely a whisper. "It took a toll on me mentally and physically, and me being this way is not healthy. My mental state is important, Blake."

She nods, her expression softening. "Ana, I can't make you do anything you don't want to do. I told you what I think, and at the end of the day, you have to do what you think is best. April told you the truth, Ana. The only thing getting in your way is you. I love the shit out of you, but I don't agree with how you're handling this situation. You're playing games and making this a much bigger mess than it needs to be, and that's not you!"

With that, she moves to the kitchen, leaving me alone with my thoughts as she orders dinner.

Even after we eat, I stay on the couch, my mind churning, trying to figure out how to approach Knox. Hours pass, but I'm no closer to finding a solution. The exhaustion of my mental battle finally overwhelms me, and I decide the only thing I can do right now is sleep on it.

It's been a few weeks since I last saw Knox. The sting of that reality has dulled slightly, but it still cuts deep, bringing tears to my eyes whenever I think about it. The silence of my room is interrupted by the faint sound of voices in the living room.

Curious, I get up and walk out, catching the tail end of a conversation between April and Blake.

"I'll tell her tonight," Blake whispers clearly, not wanting me to hear her. "She's been a mess, and I know this will only make her feel more conflicted."

"Tell me what?" I ask, stepping into the room, suspicion lacing my voice.

Blake takes a deep breath, bracing herself as April takes an audible breath. "April ran into Knox this afternoon."

My heart stops. "Oh… How is he?" The question comes out small, barely masking the dread tightening in my stomach.

"He's seeing someone he works with," Blake announces, her tone casual as if she were telling me what's for dinner. Blake and I are very similar in that respect, she doesn't mince words. These words, though, hit me like a ton of bricks. I kind of wish she would have tried to soften the blow.

"Well fuck, Blake, way to ease me into this information," I snap, irritation flaring up despite the hurt.

"Really? You want me to beat around the bush? You've been doing enough of that for everyone lately," she shoots back, walking toward her room.

The room suddenly feels colder, emptier. April shifts uncomfortably, her eyes full of sympathy. "I'm really sorry, I don't know what to say, Ana."

"I need to be alone," I respond, my voice hollow as I retreat back to my room, leaving April standing there in awkward silence.

I have no idea how long I stay locked away, the minutes blending into hours as my thoughts spiral. My mind is a mess, each thought crashing into the next, leaving me more lost and broken. I glance at my reflection in the mirror, but the person staring back at me is a stranger, a ghost of the person I used to be, a shell of someone who once believed love could be simple if you just remove the drama.

Today, March 1

"I feel darkness break upon her"
-Blink 182

Knox

T HE WORLD IS RUSHING past me, each second passing without me being able to get a steady grasp.

Ana's brother, Ryan is sitting across from me, silent. I haven't heard him say a word the entire time we've been here. I know how close they are, so I know this is killing him. I wish I had it in me to talk to him, bring him out from wherever he is hiding, lost in his own thoughts, but I can't.

I can't fucking do anything.

So, we sit here, two turtles retreated in our shells, seeking comfort from within, and based on the look on his face, he can't fucking find it either! The only thing I find any sense of comfort in, is the past, no matter how painful it was. So I continue to retreat there, in our messy past.

Summer, Two Years Ago

"Where are you?
And I'm so sorry"
- Blink 182

Ana

BLAKE HAS BEEN MY anchor through everything, the one constant that kept me from being swallowed whole by the chaos of that night. When I fell apart after the Halloween party, she was there, unflinchingly loyal. I remember her gently holding my hair back as I leaned over the toilet, unloading the contents of my stomach over and over again, and the wrenching sobs that came with it. She stayed with me through those weeks, enduring my self-destructive spiral with a patience I didn't deserve.

Her presence became a lifeline. Every time Knox's name or face haunted my thoughts, Blake was there to soothe my frayed nerves, to remind me I wasn't entirely lost. When my world turned upside down, she took charge, calling my brother and managing the practicalities so I could focus on just getting through the day.

And when my brother came to stay a few weeks later, Blake didn't hesitate to support me in any way she could. She moved in with April for three weeks to give my brother space to be there for the doctor visits and imaging appointments. Her selflessness was a balm for my shattered spirit.

So when Blake speaks, her words carry weight. They pierce through the haze of my numbness and reach the core of my soul. Ignoring her advice or brushing off her concerns feels impossible because I know, deep down, she's been the one holding me together when I couldn't hold myself.

Her words now though, charged with concern, are a mirror echoing around me. She's starting to lose patience with me. "Ana, it has been eight months since the party, five months since you've last seen him. It's time you get over yourself and tell Knox the truth. You love him and you're torturing both of you for no reason."

"I know," I respond, burying my face in my hands.

"Then go see him," Blake says. "He thinks you and Ryan are together. He deserves to know he's your brother. He deserves to know why he was here," she scolds.

"Blake," I sigh, "I tried to tell him, I tried to tell him everything, but he slammed the door in my face, LIT-ERALLY slammed it."

"He was hurt," she says. "Stop the bullshit, and go talk to him, before it's too late."

"He told me he was going to move on that night, and you heard April, he started dating some girl from work. What am I going to do Blake, walk in all Meredith Grey on his ass? *Pick me, choose me, love me,*" I mock in a high pitched voice. "No thanks, that's not me."

"He deserves the truth, Ana," she says flatly, turning her back towards me, and walking away.

She's right.

I step into the shower, letting the hot water pour over me as if I can wash away the doubts and fears gnawing at me. I wrap myself in the comforting cocoon of steam, but the thoughts of what I need to do weighs heavy on my mind.

After I finish, I grab an oversized t-shirt from the closet, letting its softness wrap around me like a shield. I pull on my favorite biker shorts, the ones that are both comfortable and familiar, and lace up my Converse.

Standing in front of the mirror, I take one last look at myself. I need to see Knox, and if I let myself dwell on it, or think about it too long, I know I'll back out. The familiar fear of confrontation will creep in, whispering all the reasons why I shouldn't go.

But I can't let that happen. I need to face this, to confront Knox and whatever is left between us. The decision is made, the only thing left is to act on it before my courage vanishes. With a deep breath, I grab my keys and head out the door, determined to push through the anxiety and see this through.

It's June in Vermont, so the air has changed from crisp and cold to a warmth that kisses your skin with a soft, golden touch. Today is a typical June day, just a few fluffy clouds and the sun shining bright. It's 80 degrees outside, perfect weather for Chinese takeout on the balcony.

Hopeful that Blake is right, and enough time has passed, I stop at the Chinese restaurant up the street from Knox's apartment and pick up the order I called and placed on my way over.

The drive felt longer than usual, each minute stretching out as I replay the conversation in my head, trying to steady my nerves. As I walk into the restaurant, the familiar scent of spices and grilled meat fills the air, providing a comforting distraction from the swirling thoughts in my mind.

I approach the counter, the staff handing me the bag with my order in it. The smell of the Chinese food, warm and inviting, does little to calm my racing heart but offers a small comfort. I check the order briefly to make sure everything's in there.

With the bag in hand, I head back to my car, trying to gather my resolve for what's to come. The drive to Knox's apartment feels like it takes forever, each turn and stop light intensifying the anticipation. The scents of chicken lo mein, sesame chicken, and wonton soup waft through the car as the air conditioner blows in my face. Finally, I pull up to his building, my breath coming in shallow bursts.

Getting out of the car is hard with my back being as sore as it is on the daily, and I'm moving a lot slower. I bend down, grabbing my purse, the bag of takeout, and the bottle of soda from the passenger seat and make my way up the sidewalk towards the door of Knox's building.

As I approach the building, my rehearsed lines play in my mind, a futile attempt to prepare for what I'm about to face. But as I get closer, my thoughts crumble, and my heart begins to pound so violently it feels like it might break free from my chest. I can hardly breathe.

And there, right in front of me, Knox is walking beside a tall blonde. They're both carrying what looks like personal belongings, likely from the U-Haul parked on the street. The sight hits me like a punch to the gut: He's not just seeing someone from work. She's moving in…

The realization sends shockwaves through me, making my legs feel like lead. I stand frozen for a moment, the bag of Chinese food feeling impossibly heavy in my hand. The warmth and comfort I hoped to bring are overshadowed by the raw, stinging pain of seeing him with someone else.

I watch as they carry boxes and bags towards the building, Knox's face lit up with a smile I remember so vividly from our own time together. The sight of his happiness, now shared with someone else, feels like a knife twisting deeper into the wound.

I'm standing here, caught in a whirlwind of emotions, betrayal, sadness, anger. Every reason I had for coming here seems irrelevant now. The thought of confronting him seems impossible in this moment of overwhelming hurt.

I take a step back, wanting to hide before he sees me, before I have to face this new reality head-on.

He loves her.

I know Knox falls fast, I felt it when we were together. He doesn't want to be alone.

Why does he always dive head first? The thought is accompanied with a bitter edge.

Does Knox's heart just leap from one intense infatuation to the next, barely pausing to catch its breath? Does he need the rush of love to feel alive, to fill the void he has? It makes me question the depth of the feelings he once had for me. Was I just another chapter in his book of fleeting romance?

My mind flashes back to my time with Knox, the days he seemed so sure, so devoted, the days I believed he loved me. I believed in it enough to let him sweep me away. But now, seeing he has fallen for *her*, I can't help but feel a pang of resentment. I know I did this, but what we had feels cheapened, and less special as I stand here watching him start a new story with someone else.

Is this what he felt when he saw me with Ryan?

The crushing blow, when the person you love is falling in love with someone else? A deep sense of loss, and heartache as you watch the future you want dissolve right in front of you?

I miss you! I miss you so much, it is killing me. Every day I'm in a constant battle with myself. Brutally serving as a reminder I failed us and made a stupid choice. I'm so pissed at myself for letting my fear rob us of time together, of being so careless and childish. I want to be with you, no more bullshit. Just us. Knox, Please be with me.

That's what I wanted to say, that's what I've been rehearsing in my head. I'm so naive. I thought I would show up here, say those words, tell him the truth, all of it, and then we would spend the rest of the night sweaty, tangled in bed, wrapped up in one another.

Instead I turn around, put everything back in my car, get in the driver's seat, and start to cry.

Knox

I SAW HER AGAIN. Outside, just now. It was brief, and it took my goddam breath away, but I can't give in. I can't let myself wonder why she came here. I have to let myself move on. I was a broken mess when I met Ana. I was literally on the verge of self destruction, and she put me back together stitch by stitch. She gave me something to look forward to, helped me find purpose, a new path. She helped me feel again. It was quick, only a month, but there was a consuming intensity, something I've never felt with anyone else.

I firmly believe people enter our lives for a reason, and sometimes that reason is not to stay. They come into our lives to teach us, support us, shape our journey in ways we never knew we needed and may not fully understand. Without them our path would be completely different. Their presence, while temporary, serves a crucial role in providing lessons, growth, and even moments of joy. But sometimes we mistake their role in our story, wanting to hold on so they will stay longer, and when they don't, the pain is swift.

That could be Ana. She put me back together, but I can't let her break me back apart.

She moved on.

She forgot me.

She loves someone else.

Falling in love with Mia was nothing like it was with Ana. It was gradual, and so subtle I almost missed the signs. At first it was easy to overlook the growing affection I felt for her, as it quietly developed below the surface. It wasn't until I let go of Ana after she showed up at my door that night, and truly faced my emotions when I realized how deeply I had come to care for Mia in the time we had been working together. Mia started just a few weeks after me. What started gradual and understated, became unmistakably clear once the weight of the past was lifted revealing a strong genuine connection I hadn't acknowledged before.

It started with small everyday interactions. We laughed over casual conversations and mutual support on little side projects at work. Over time, those moments of connection grew. Those simple acts of sounding out ideas together and the comfort I felt around her quietly built a foundation of affection. Slowly, she occupied my thoughts, and I looked forward to seeing her.

Our first date was simple, and short. We decided to get a cup of coffee after work. We talked and laughed, sharing stories, and we quickly realized how much we had in common. After that, we decided to take a walk.

I love her, and after everything with Ana, I decided time is not always kind, so why not make the move? Ana moved on, so I needed to try to move on too, and Mia is someone I could see myself with.

My thoughts bring me back to the day I asked Mia to move in with me.

Sitting across from Mia at our coffee shop, the cozy atmosphere filled with the aroma of freshly brewed coffee and a soft hum of conversation. When I looked at her, my heart pounded. Ethan had just landed a new job and planned to move soon. It felt like the perfect opportunity to ask Mia to move in with me, even if it was fast.

"Mia," I began, my voice steady, but hands trembling. "I know we haven't been together very long, but Ethan is moving out soon, and well, I've been thinking about us."

Mia looked up from her coffee, her eyes now curious. "Is that so? What have you been thinking?"

I took a deep breath, "I know it's only been two months, and I know I probably sound fucking crazy, but being with you just feels right. I don't want to wait around or overthink it, I want you to move in with me."

She blinked, surprised, a smile playing at the corners of her lips. "You're serious?"

"Fuck yeah, I am. Love with you is different than anything I have ever felt, Mia. It's easy. I know it's soon, but I'm tired of missing out on shit in my life because of timing."

She sat across from me taking another drink of her coffee, just staring at me for what felt like hours. I could see the thoughts zooming through her mind, and then finally she looked at me.

"Knox, this is really crazy," she laughed, "But ok, let's do it!"

I remember feeling so excited. We sipped our coffee, and started making plans. I couldn't wait for her to move in.

So, this is where I have to be right now, with my mind on Mia, in the present.

Not with Ana in the past.

After we unpacked all of Mia's things, we celebrated our new life together christening every surface in the apartment.

Sex with Ana was intense, and urgent, a whirlwind of passion consuming every moment with fiery intensity. It was exhilarating and immediate, driven by a powerful, almost overwhelming desire. With Mia, it's softer, sincere, a serene experience providing warmth and comfort. It's the kind of sex I never thought I'd want, but I'm here for it. She taught me how to balance urgency and peace. I'm different with her, softer.

I loved and needed Ana more than I needed my next breath, but fate failed us, and I can't go back and let her be my undoing… again.

March 2

"I'll take you over if you let me"
-Blink 182

<h1 style="text-align:center">Ana</h1>

"HI, BABY. IT'S MOM." My mom's voice is soft, trembling with a mixture of hope and sorrow. "I know you can hear me. I can feel it deep in my bones."

She pauses, as if searching for the right words to make me believe, like she does, that everything will be okay. "Mamas always know their babies. You're an extension of me," Her voice cracks slightly, betraying the strength she's trying so hard to maintain. "We're all here, waiting for you to wake up. I love you, baby. I'll be right here all night, just in case."

I can hear her. It's just out of reach, like a memory from a dream, but her voice cuts through the fog clouding my mind. There's sadness in her tone, a deep, aching sorrow making me want to reach out and comfort her, to tell her I'm here.

I'm here, Mom. I can hear you. I'm here, I just . . . can't reach you.

I scream the words in my head, desperate to break through the barrier that's keeping us apart. I want to move, to open my eyes, to give her any sign I'm still here, that I haven't left her. But no matter how hard I try, my body betrays me. It's like I'm trapped, sinking further and further into a darkness pulling me away from her, away from the world.

I fight against it, straining to lift even a finger, to force my lips to move, but it's no use. The darkness is relentless, dragging me under, and all the sounds, the beeping machines, the quiet murmurs of the nurses, even my mother's tearful whispers, fade away into nothingness.

The silence is deafening. It wraps around me like a suffocating blanket, drowning out the last remnants of light and hope. I want to cry out, to tell my mom not to give up, that I'm still fighting, but the words are lost in the void, swallowed up by the overwhelming emptiness.

Please, Mom… don't stop talking to me. I'm still here. I just can't…

But the thought drifts away, slipping through my grasp as the darkness pulls me deeper, until there's nothing left but silence.

Summer, Two Years Ago

"This is growing up"
-Blink 182

Ana

T IME HAS SLIPPED THROUGH my fingers like fine grains of sand, and the reality of my situation is becoming harder to ignore. I'm running out of time, and I can feel the weight of the impending changes pressing down on me. The future and my fate, is staring me right in the face, and the sense of urgency is almost suffocating.

Blake's words echo in my mind, each one a harsh reminder of the choices I've made and the consequences I now face. She was right about everything. She warned me, tried to guide me through the chaos, but I was too stubborn to listen, and too wrapped up in my own mistakes to see it clearly.

As I look ahead, the path is becoming clearer. The decisions I make now will shape the rest of my life. In just a few weeks, everything will change. I've tried to reach out, to fix what's been broken, but it seems like every attempt only drops me deeper into the hole I've dug.

As the days tick away, I find myself grappling with the weight of the choices I need to make. The future is no longer a distant concern, it's an imminent reality quickly approaching. One I can no longer avoid. The fear of making the wrong decision is fucking paralyzing.

In these final weeks, I'm forced to confront the truth.

I should have told him three months ago. Fuck, I should have stayed and made him listen. But I didn't, and now he's with her, and I'm alone. I'm alone, and I can't do this alone. I can't.

The weight of regret is almost unbearable. Every passing day feels like a fresh stab in the gut.

Seeing him with someone else feels like a cruel twist of fate. He's moved on, and I'm left picking up the pieces of my shattered heart. The emptiness filling my days is overwhelming. I find myself staring blankly at the walls, lost in thoughts of what could have been, what should have been.

The loneliness is a thick fog clinging to every corner of my life, making everything feel heavy and dark. I try to distract myself, to focus on work and other responsibilities, but the loneliness seeps through, a constant reminder of how alone I really am.

Nothing can fill the void that is Knox Fucking Reed. I need him, and I don't know how to cope without him. The nights are the hardest. I lie awake in bed, staring at the ceiling, my thoughts consumed by the memories of us. I can't escape the longing for what we had, the way he made me feel whole.

I feel like I'm stuck in limbo, unable to move forward and unwilling to go back. I want to scream, to lash out at the world for being so unfair, but all I can do is sit in silence, grappling with the pain. I'm caught in a cycle of self-pity and regret, unable to find a way out. This is not me, this is not who I am.

I need him back. I need to make things right. But I also know I might be too late, and the thought is almost more than I can bear. Why does she get him and I don't?

I can't continue to sit idly by, so I get out a pen and paper, and I write.

Knox,

I know this is going to be difficult to read, but there is something incredibly important I need to tell you. You have no idea how much I hate myself right now, that I haven't been able to say this to you in person.

I'm pregnant, with your baby, and I'm due in a few weeks.

I'm sorry for being so blunt, but you know me, no bullshit. I know it has taken me too long to tell you, and I regret every second that you haven't known.

I tried so hard to tell you that night I came to your apartment, but you were so hurt and upset, and when you closed the door on me, I didn't know how to come back with the right words. I was overwhelmed with fear and confusion, and I just couldn't bring myself to speak up.

I want to clear something up that I know has hurt you. The guy you saw me with is not someone I fell in love with, Knox; he's my brother, Ryan. After everything that happened with April, I was scared and lost. I found out I was having a baby, and then April came to see me, it was so much to take in at one time. Blake was there for me, and she called Ryan. He came and stayed with me for three weeks so he could go with me to my doctor appointments and ultrasound. He didn't want me to go alone, and I didn't know what to tell my parents. It should have been you by my side, I should have told you sooner. I know I've taken so much from you, our future, our chance to be a family.

Knox, I'm so sorry.

I came to tell you in person, but when I saw you moving in with someone new, I realized it wasn't the right time either. You seemed so happy and I didn't want to blow up your world.

I decided to write this letter, because it seems like fate fucking hates us, and I want you to know that despite everything, I hope you will be there for the birth of our child. I understand if you can't forgive me, but I need you to know the truth. Our son needs you in his life, Knox. We are having a boy. I want you there for everything, no matter how it unfolds.

Call me or come see me when you're ready.

−Ana

After I finish writing the letter, I place it in an envelope, seal it shut and scroll Knox's name across the front.

I can't keep avoiding this any longer. I have to tell him what is going on. I have never had anxiety like this. My hormones are all over the place, and the fear I have of rejection for Knox is overwhelming. Needing to calm my nerves, I change into my yoga pants, grab my yoga mat and place it by the door. I have to recenter myself so I actually follow through with telling Knox and I don't chicken out.

I think back on the day I found out I was pregnant.

My period has always been unpredictable, so I didn't really think much of not having one. It happened all the time. One morning Blake made us chocolate banana smoothies, usually one of my favorites.

"Why does this smell weird?" I asked her as she handed it to me.

Smelling it she said, "It smells fine to me."

As I brought it closer to my lips, the intense smell of peanut butter hit my nose, and I pushed it away. "No, it's too strong."

"Well, I spent the last 15 minutes making it, so the least you can do is take a sip," Blake said to me, annoyed.

I brought it to my mouth and took a sip. On the way down, a piece of banana not blended completely hit the back of my throat and I projectile vomited all over the kitchen floor.

"Ana, you've been nauseous a lot lately, and now you're puking and have the nose of a canine. Maybe you need to take a pregnancy test," Blake commented with concern as she grabbed a washrag from the sink.

I waited two more days, and when the nausea didn't subside, I called Blake and asked her to go to the store with me to get a test.

"Peeing on a stick is the most stressful thing I have ever done!" I told Blake as she pulled off the towel I placed over the test to hide it from my view while it percolated for the required two minutes.

Her face was unreadable as she handed the test to me. I immediately started to sob. What am I going to do? He slept with someone else, and now I'm having his baby!

It wasn't until after I found out I was pregnant April came by and told me what actually happened at the

Halloween party. By then I was so scared and had no idea how to move forward, so I retreated, trying to wrap my head around everything. Then by the time I got the nerve to tell him, he was seeing someone else. Why is time not on our side?

Deciding I need a little encouragement, I pick up the phone and call Ryan. He has been in this with me since the beginning, and I need a little male perspective. The phone rings twice before he picks up.

"Hey, what's up?" he asks casually.

"I'm freaking the fuck out, Ryan. I went by Knox's to try for the second time to tell him I'm pregnant and he was with his new girlfriend."

"Did she answer the door?" he asks.

"No, they were outside the building, carrying her boxes from a U-Haul to his apartment. She was moving in, Ryan."

"What did you say?"

"I didn't say anything. I got back in my car and left before they saw me."

"He still doesn't know." It's not a question, he knows the answer. "You have to tell him Ana."

"I know Ryan, but apparently I can't do it in person. So I wrote him a letter."

"You're going to tell the guy who knocked you up that you're having his baby in a letter? That's a terrible fucking idea, Sis."

"Thanks for the pep talk," I respond flatly.

"It's not my job to give you a pep talk right now, I'm supposed to protect you, and keep it real. This is not a good idea. Go knock on his door and tell him face to face like a goddamn adult, Ana."

"What about *her*?"

"This isn't about her," he says.

"No, I can't. I gotta go," I say hanging up, grabbing my bag and heading out the door.

I'm going to slide it under the doormat and then go unwind at yoga for pregnant moms.

Knox

"Coffee smells amazing, sweets," I say, rubbing the sleep from my eyes as I walk into the kitchen. Instead of seeing Mia cocooned in a gentle cloud of sleepiness, I find an empty kitchen aside from a little pink post-it and an envelope with my name scrolled in tight letters across the front.

Pouring a cup of coffee, I settle into a comfortable spot, taking a moment to carefully read the post-it before even touching the envelope it was attached to.

> Knoxie,
>
> I completely forgot about my hair appointment this morning after the _fun_ we had last night. Just found this envelope under the doormat. I guess we will have to pick up where we left off in a few hours.
>
> See you soon!

Picking up the envelope, a smile tugs my lips as I remember the fun Mia was referring to. The image of us, tangled in sheets and lost in each other, makes my cock stir to life. The sensation of her warm breath against my neck, and the way we explored every inch of each other's skin, it all comes rushing back. I feel the lingering touch, the playful kisses and I hear her moan my name. I chuckle as I unfold the letter.

In contrast to my memories of last night, the letter delivers a wicked punch. The second I open it, five words sitting alone in the middle of two separate paragraphs jump out at me before I even read a word, like they were deliberately placed there:

"I'm pregnant with your baby."

The room immediately seems to spin around me. I can't bring myself to read the rest of the letter. I get up and move to the couch, staring at the five words. My palms sweaty, my heart racing. I sit and stare, unable to read anything else on the page.

After an indiscernible amount of time, I move to the bathroom, and turn on the shower. The water is pelting my skin making it tingle with each drop. I stand there lost in my thoughts, mind racing, until the water runs cold.

I get out of the shower, dry off, and then I turn on the TV. I'm not sure what's on, I can't focus on anything but the five words mocking me. Is this a cruel joke?

I stare at those words for an hour and a half. Each time I reread them, memories with Ana fill my brain… The realization hits me with a cold shock, using a condom had never even occurred to us. I hadn't realized until now how reckless we had been. The weight of it all is overwhelming, the gravity of the situation pressing heavy on my chest.

How could something as basic as a fucking condom never have even crossed our minds? It's as if they simply didn't exist in our reality. We never even mentioned them, not before, not during, not after. NEVER!

Mia.

Shit, Mia.

Turmoil sets in as I find myself torn between the urgent need to figure out how the hell to tell Mia and the pressing desire to read the rest of the letter. My thoughts churn in chaos, unable to settle on a single course of action.

Finally, after pacing the room for confirmation of what my next move should be, I force myself to read the rest of the letter, the situation only grows worse and more complicated the more I read. Ana hadn't fallen in love with someone else, she tried to tell me, but I was too hurt and angry to listen. She reached out, confused and frightened, and I slammed the motherfucking door in her face.

She didn't move on.

She didn't forget me.

She didn't fall in love with someone else.

This changes everything!

I was consumed by her from the moment I saw her that night at the bar. She was pure fucking perfection in my mind from the second I opened my eyes and they landed on her. From the first second, I had a clear craving. I would have turned the world upside down to keep her, and now I'm sitting here split in half: Mia, who has become more to me than I ever thought she could be, and Ana, Stitch, the woman carrying my child and who would always hold a special place in my heart. The weight of it all feels fucking unbearable, and I'm buried underneath layers of guilt and confusion. Trying to sort through my feelings for them both seems like a betrayal, a knife twisting in my gut. What am I going to do, how do I want to try and move forward from here?

Mia is my rock, my steady anchor in the storm. She was there when Ana left me hanging out to dry. Our life together is comfortable and filled with love. She is making a home for us, supporting me in ways I didn't realize I needed, and every day with her feels like a gift. Do I really love her with the same intensity? Am I in love with her, or the idea of what she brings to my life? I feel like such a bastard for putting her in this position.

But then there's Ana. Fucking, Anabelle Scott. The way she makes my heart race with just a look, the way she makes me feel, from my heart to my cock, the memories are still so vivid. Knowing she's carrying my child, and isn't seeing someone else makes everything more complicated. I originally moved on because I thought I had to. Now what? It's a life I helped create, and the responsibility weighs heavily on me. I can't just walk away from this. The thought of not being there for her, for our child, is fucking unbearable. Again, the idea I closed the door on us, moved on because I was sure she was no longer an option haunts me.

The guilt is overwhelming, and I can't shake the feeling that no matter what choice I make, someone will be hurt. Staying with Mia feels like I'm abandoning Ana and our child, all possibilities of us being a family. Choosing to fight for a relationship with Ana even if it doesn't end in us together, feels like disregarding Mia. Each path is a waiting disaster, and I'm caught in the middle, unable to see a way forward that doesn't involve breaking someone's fucking heart.

The emotions swirl around me like a torrent. I'm trapped in a cycle of guilt and confusion, each decision weighing on me more heavily than the last. It's like being pulled in two directions at once, each choice tearing at my heart and soul.

I wish I could find a clear path, a way to make this right for everyone involved. But right now, all I can do is sit here, feeling like I'm drowning. The love I feel for both Mia and Ana is real, but fuck, it's tearing me apart. In the end, it feels like no matter what I choose, I'm fucked. The weight of it all is crushing, and I'm left feeling powerless, caught between the love I have and the love I *had*, one including a responsibility I can't ignore.

I asked Mia to meet me at our coffee shop. I know it seems cruel to taint the place we love, with words that will shatter her completely, but I can't tell her in our home. In the very same place Ana and I likely conceived our son.

My words are lead in my mouth, but I know I have to be honest and straightforward no matter how painful it may be.

As soon as she walks in she runs to me, placing a chaste kiss on my lips, twirling around so I can see her new hairstyle. She cut a good 6 inches off the length and added some soft highlights around her face. She's glowing. She looks so happy, and I'm about to burst the little bubble we have been living in with a motherfucking sledgehammer. I wince at the thought.

I begin, my voice heavy with emotion, "Mia, there is something, " I struggle to keep my tone steady. "It's about the letter you left on the counter, it was from Ana. It's… dammit."

Her entire body shifts with my words, becoming stone cold right before my eyes. The light that was there when she walked in has flickered out like the flame on the end of a match. Her smile dissolves into a cold stare, and her hands are trembling as she reaches for her drink.

I pause trying to gauge her reaction before continuing, "Ana's pregnant, and the baby is mine." I can't even pause to give her a second to register the blow, if I do, I won't finish, so I charge on. "She's been trying to reach me, since she found out, before you and I were dating, and

I wouldn't listen." Her expression is unreadable. "I know this is a lot," I continue, my voice breaking. "I love you, Mia, but I'm also going to be a father any day now and I don't know what that means for us. I wanted you to hear it from me. I couldn't keep this shit from you."

The weight of my confession hangs heavy in the air, my heart aching as I watch Mia from across the table. Hoping she understands.

Her face pales as she processes my words, the gravity of the situation settling in. Tears well up in her eyes, and her voice trembles as she speaks. "I don't know what to say Knox," she says softly, almost as if she's trying to make sense of it herself.

"How did this happen?" She waves her hand in the air, "Don't answer that, it's a stupid question."

I reach out for her hand on the edge of the table, and she pulls it away, placing it in her lap. "Do you love her? Do you want to be with her?"

"Mia, I can't lie to you, it wouldn't be fair, but that's a loaded fucking question. I loved her the second I laid eyes on her, but I also love you more than I can express right now. I am with *you*. This doesn't have to change that."

"But if it did, would you be with her?"

"Maybe," I sigh, "I don't know. I have no fucking clue. A lot has happened between us. We're not who we used to be."

"Will you change your mind?

"Mia, I have no clue what will happen," I grunt in frustration. "She's having my baby. A baby made out of love, but that love morphed and changed and turned into something resembling hate. I don't want to bring a baby into that shit. I don't believe in staying together for the kids. I know that doesn't make you feel better, but it's the truth."

"But… never mind." She pauses, taking a shaky breath. "I love you, Knox, but I'm not sure if I will be able to watch someone else make you a father." She pauses again for a long second and lets out another shaky breath with tears falling down her face. "But, I guess life isn't always simple. I want to be here with you. I want to work through this together, but I can't promise it won't change as we get deeper in this."

"Ok." I get out of my chair and bend down on the floor next to her, grabbing her hand and smothering it with little kisses. "That's ok, this is more than I deserve from you."

Her words hang in the air, heavy with the weight of what's at stake. The sincerity in her eyes and the vulnerability in her voice make it clear how much she loves me.

In this moment, I see the depth of her commitment and the strength of her feelings. It's a bittersweet reminder of what we have together, and it makes this so much harder. Her willingness to face the shitshow of mine and Ana's situation head-on is both a relief and a fucking curse.

Mia is asleep on my chest, her head resting softly against me, her breaths deep and even in the quiet of the night. Despite the shock of everything that's happened, she's here with me, offering unwavering love in the midst of a shit ton of chaos. We'd spent the earlier part of the day wrapped in the heavy weight of our conversations, drinking coffee and trying to piece together how to move forward.

Earlier, at the cafe, her tears mingled with the steam of our coffee as we talked, the sound of her sobs punctuating our attempts to navigate the uncertainty of our situation. It was a difficult conversation, filled with raw emotion and strained effort to find a path forward. Her pain was palpable, and every word felt like an additional weight pressing down on both of us.

We left her car at the café, she was too overwhelmed to drive, and she cried the entire way home. Her tears fell silently, a steady stream mirroring the turmoil inside her. When we finally arrived back home, the quiet of the house seemed to echo her grief, and she cried herself to sleep, curled up beside me.

Now, as she sleeps, her presence is a balm to my frayed nerves. The weight of our conversation and the gravity of the decisions I have to make feels slightly lighter now that we're home, in our home, and she is still here with me. Even in the midst of all this bullshit, her love and commitment is crystal clear.

I'm left alone with my thoughts as she sleeps, once again trying to reconcile the complexity of my feelings for both Mia and Ana. I love them both deeply, but obviously Ana doesn't want to be with me. Do I try anyways? I find myself torn between trying to reconcile with Ana, in an effort to build a family for our child, and staying with Mia, who even through the broken shards of her heart, is unwavering. Then there is the unspoken truth evoking feelings I can't register: Ana probably doesn't have feelings for me at all, she might not want me back after all that has happened, and Mia might decide this is all too much. My entire fate is out of my hands, and still, it feels like a never-ending battle whirling inside my head. Mia's support and understanding, despite the pain, make it evident how much she cares and how willing she is to face these challenges with me. How do I walk away after she was so willing to support me through this? Is it even fair to bring her along on this fucked up rollercoaster?

The future feels uncertain and full of difficulty, but in this quiet moment, I hold onto the hope somehow, we'll find a way through this.

Thoughts are running like rapid fire through my mind, all over the fucking place, seeming to play on repeat. I carefully slide out from beneath Mia. I move and sit on the edge of my bed with my head in my hands, and count. A coping strategy my therapist taught me to re-center and ground myself when my anxious thoughts take over and my desire to numb becomes overwhelming. A strategy I am clinging to like a lifeline at this moment.

I count, and despite the long conversation with Mia and my love for her, my thoughts can't help but drift to Ana.

I count.

Five things I can see:

One… the balcony Ana decorated for Halloween

Two… the empty space where her chair used to sit

Three… the dark green blanket we made love under that I couldn't bring myself to throw out

Four… the black hoodie on my floor that is her favorite

Five… the TV that played her favorite movies when it rained

Four things I can touch or feel:

One… The blankets covering the bed we most likely made a baby in

Two… the carpet I laid her on more times than I can count

Three… the lamp I used to turn on so I could see her naked underneath me

Four… my heart breaking

Three things I can hear:

One… her laugh on our first date

Two… her cries on the night I slammed the door in her face

Three… her moaning my name

Two things I can smell:

One… maple

Two… lavender

One thing I can taste:

Her…

She's unraveling each stitch she wove, she's taking it all back.

I missed it all. My mind is playing tricks on me as I let it drift painfully to a what-if scenario.

"Knox," Ana whimpers as I place kisses across her shoulder blades. We've been sitting in the cozy corner of my room cuddled in this chair for about an hour. "Knox, I can't believe we're having a baby. A baby, Knox." Her voice is quiet, laced with a mixture of excitement and fear.

"Me either, Stitch. I can't wait to see you all fat, and swollen with my baby inside you. Shit, that's so hot. The idea of you being full of me, makes me so fucking turned on."

"Why do you have to make it gross?"

"It's not gross. It's sexy as hell."

"Every mom I know talks about the stretch marks they have all over their stomach and boobs and ass," she winces. "That's going to be me, the deflated balloon holding your baby."

"Those marks will just be evidence you're mine, Stitch. They'll belong to me. I put them there, marked you! Fuck, that's sexy," I tell her.

"You know," I add, nipping at her neck "I can't get you more pregnant than you already are."

"Mmhmm," she moans.

With that small voice of approval I carry her to the bed kissing her all over as I undress her, stopping at her belly, kissing it with more love than I ever thought I could hold.

I stopped my thoughts there, not wanting to venture too far into dangerous waters. She brings out the most carnal side of me. Guilt sets in as I sit here, unable to deny the attraction to the idea of Ana as the mother of my child as I look over my shoulder at Mia still asleep in my bed.

Do I even want her to be a part of this? Why am I so unsure of her place in all of this? Shouldn't it be more clear? This isn't fair to her. I can't stay with her just because she's willing to trudge through this with me and I don't want to hurt her. I should stay with her because I love her more than anything, but I don't know if that's true. If it was, I wouldn't be drifting to thoughts of Ana. I'm not sure deep down I love her the way I should. We really need to talk.

Fuck!

Pushing the thoughts away to the far back corner of my brain, too tired to truly process my thoughts and feelings, I stand up, put on my sweats and a hoodie and walk out into the living room. I need to escape the memories surrounding me in that motherfucking bedroom. After I thought Ana had moved on, I realized being ghosted by her wasn't ending anytime soon, so I packed up her cozy corner in my room. I couldn't stand to look at it for another goddamn second. It was a terrible reminder of everything we had, and of everything that went wrong.

Guess getting rid of the shit doesn't completely cleanse the space like I had hoped it would.

I stand next to the window and look out at the dark sky. What am I going to do? How involved will I get to be? What kind of dad do I want to be? What kind of dad will she let me be?

Shaking my head I let out a long breath. I'm trying to paint her as a monster, but I know Ana, I know her heart. She will be everything to both me and our baby, whatever I need her to be, she will be. I have to remember the woman I made a baby with, the woman I loved with so much passion. I can't let my thoughts take over to make this easier on me. I can't spiral down a rabbit hole that doesn't exist, but I am spiraling.

I'm spiraling hard and fast.

Down.

Down.

Down.

After a sleepless night, I decided the only thing I could do was face this situation head on, and I have to take it one conversation at a time. Regardless of how I'm feeling, the turmoil and confusion racing around in my head, *Ana* is having my baby. And soon.

After I talk to Ana, I'll confront the inevitable with Mia.

I have already missed everything up to this point. Every fucking doctor appointment, late night craving, the first kick, the day she found out, everything.

I'm not fucking missing the rest!

I just have to find a way to get past the hate swirling around inside me, brewing in the depths of my soul, churning with intense anger and bitterness.

Hate for her.

Hate for me.

It is consuming my thoughts, tightening my chest and igniting a relentless, fiery energy seeking an outlet, leaving me feeling on edge and overwhelmed by it all.

Right alongside the hate I feel, is an equally powerful love. A love that feels like it could never flicker out. I'm going to be a dad! It permeates my thoughts, expanding my heart with an overwhelming tenderness and a deep connection to Ana.

I wish I really could just hate her. It would be so much easier, so simple. It would be a straightforward reaction to the bullshit going on, the unresolved feelings. Hatred offers a clear, albeit negative, focus and can feel like a form of emotional closure, shielding me from the vulnerability and the complexities that come with love and forgiveness. It requires less of me. Less effort, and it would be easier than working through the nuances of my emotions, than rebuilding.

My thoughts are all over the place. I was so sure before I found out, so sure of what I wanted, who I wanted to be with, what the fuck I wanted to do! Now that I'm walking up to Ana's door, I feel like such a total cocksucker, not knowing what the fuck I want!

These thoughts attack my brain like a tsunami as I push the button to ring Ana's doorbell.

I stand there for a few minutes, not even sure she is home. I am becoming more unsteady on my feet with every passing second. Unsure of what to say, void of clarity, and then Ana opens the door.

An electric shock jolts through my entire body. Ana is standing there with her hair cascading in soft waves around her shoulders, glistening under the dim morning light. I love her like this, sleep still on her face, not quite ready to face the day.

Fuck.

Her eyes are expressive, reflecting a mix of vulnerability and strength. The gentle curve of her swollen belly accentuates her radiant glow, filled with me and with her, a life we created together. My body reacts with desire, and I find myself readjusting, the action not going unnoticed by Ana.

Yet, this same sight stirs a deep, consuming hatred of unresolved pain. Her radiant beauty against my inner turmoil leaves me paralyzed. Ana speaks first, her voice resonant with emotion, "Knox," her eyes searching my face for any sign of what I might be feeling. "I… I didn't…" Her words trail off, her hand gently resting on her belly, a protective gesture that underscores her vulnerability as she invites me in. Closing the door behind her and leading me to the living room she speaks softly. "There is so much I need to explain, Knox. I'm so sorry! I should have done a million things differently." Her words hang in the air laden with unspoken history and the weight of the moment. My heart wrestles with a powerful surge of love and hate combined.

"No shit," I reply, my voice edged with bitterness, struggling to keep my emotions in check. "You think I didn't deserve some answers?" I continue feeling a mix of anger and longing, the war I'm sure is clear in my gaze.

Her eyes fill with tears, breaking my heart in two. With a tremble in her voice she begins to speak again, "Knox, please you have to understand…"

I sharply interrupt. "Understand? Understand what, Ana? That you thought I fucked April, didn't know me better and assumed the worst. That all the time we spent together, who you knew I was, was less convincing than what you *thought* you saw? Then you found out you were pregnant, and you fucking let me think you moved on, that you left me. We could have been together all this fucking time! So, what do you want from me? Do you just expect me to leave Mia? Pretend she never happened?" My frustration boils over, my words laced with pain and confusion I don't even mean, I already decided I have to let Mia go. Now I'm just saying shit to be a dick. Letting my emotions take control. "You think it's that fucking simple? That you'd write me a letter and I'd come here, and what? Make love to you? Leave behind the life I've since built for myself?"

What is wrong with me?

Pain scores her face, but quickly morphs into anger as she yells, "This is the fucking problem, Knox! This is how we got here! Every time I have tried to tell you, you interrupt me, demanding answers, but never actually allow me to give them to you!" Her voice shakes with fury and desperation, echoing the unresolved tension between us. "How can you expect to understand anything if you won't even listen?" She pauses just a second, and then continues, each word a blow to my already fragile heart. "I don't need you, Knox!" she cries, her voice breaking, desperate for me to hear it. "I've been doing this on my own the entire time, but I want you to be here. I've fucking tried, Knox, I've tried to make you a part of this, but you wouldn't hear me out. Should I have tried harder? Yes! Should I have made you listen? Yes! But I was fucking scared, Knox! I've never done this before! I've never been in a situation where I had to move through the internal battle of slut shaming myself for having sex with you raw over and over again without protection even though I know better, especially when I thought you just turned around and screwed April! What did you expect me to believe, you walked out of the bathroom actively adjusting your pants, and her tits were out for everyone to see! Tell me what I should have believed? What would you have believed if the roles had been reversed?" Her tears are flowing freely now, her shoulders shaking with the weight of her emotions. "You jumped to conclusions when you saw me with my BROTHER, Knox, and now you're in love. You went and fell in love with someone else! How could you? How, " Her words die out, her sobs uncontrollable.

YOU fucking jumped to conclusions first! That's what made this mess!

The thoughts come and fade away just as quickly as they came, watching her crumble in front of me. What the fuck am I doing? She's pregnant. This isn't good for her, it's definitely not good for our baby. I can't leave her like this. My conflicting emotions are my burden to bear. Now is not the time, she needs me to be a better man, our baby needs a better fucking man. What if the baby can hear this? I take a deep breath and pause for a moment, trying to pull together the frayed edges of my heart, just enough to be the man they both deserve.

"Anabelle." Her name leaving my lips stirs something inside me. Anger, love, desire. I miss her so fucking much. She doesn't respond, she doesn't even hear me over her cries. She is curled up sitting in the chair playing with the frayed edges of a blanket, pulling at the threads, like the ones in my chest. Holding on as if it's the only armor she has. "Anabelle," I repeat as I move to bend down in front of her.

Her eyes, red and swollen, filled with tears, find mine. She's still there. There's my girl. Just then something inside me snaps. Before I can think better of it, my lips are on hers. We are frantic, tongues tangled in deep desire, teeth clanking. Our kisses used to be smooth, as if rehearsed even in moments of passion, so in sync we could navigate the heated exchange as if we were gliding on glass. This kiss is messy, unrehearsed, barreling into one another without actually making consistent contact. Our hands are both scratching, pulling, landing everywhere and nowhere in particular. My dick stirs to life, pressing against the zipper of my pants, pain radiating from the tip, as I continue to kiss her in this chaotic collision of lips, teeth, and tangled emotions. It's messy and imperfect, yet electrifying, as the raw intensity of our feelings spills over into every fucking touch.

I pull her hair, extending her neck back to grant myself better access. Biting and kissing the length of her neck.

"Knox! I can't… I can't stop this. You have to stop this." she pants.

"Shut the fuck up Ana!" I demand pulling her mouth back to mine. This time we find our rhythm. I palm her breasts, noting the sizable difference since the last time they were in my hands. They're larger, fuller, firmer.

"Knox, wait! I can't, I'm not that chick, I refuse to be the other woman! Knox does she know? Tell me she knows!" she cries.

Shit!

I pull away abruptly, my breaths heavy and my face filled with regret. "I'm sorry", I say looking at her. "Fuck!" I yell. "Goddamit, I shouldn't be doing this," I say in a heavy voice, rearranging my dick for the second time since I've been here. I'm such a piece of shit! "I have to go talk to Mia, tell her what a piece of shit I am. Ana, I fucking love you, I've always loved you. Seeing you, pregnant with my baby is a dream clearly stirring emotions in me. But there is so much here. So much hurt, and destruction. I have no control when it comes to you. Look at me! This is the first conversation we've had in months and I cheated on my girlfriend after I asked her to move in with me. Clearly my love for her is not what I thought it was, and I can't string her along. She's so good, so fucking good, and FUCK! She doesn't deserve this." I take a long breath trying to piece together my frayed nerves. "But you're right, you're not the other woman, and you and I can't do this either, this frantic burning desire stirred by sex and passion. That's not what you are to me, Ana, you're more than sex. I have to go. I'll be here for you and the baby, but I… I need to go."

Without another word I turn and walk out of Ana's apartment, panic overtaking my every motion as I sink further into feeling like a piece of shit! The clang of the door echoes in the dark, empty hallway. I have always fucked around, but cheating is not me! Cheating is something I despise, and shame on me for putting Ana in this position knowing her struggle with her dad cheating! I hate myself right now!

Fuck! Fuck! Fuck! What the hell did I just do? What the fuck happened? I can't believe I let myself lose all control and fucked this up even more!

The elevator dings and I turn, my heart racing with an adrenaline-fueled panic. Ana bursts out into the hallway, her face a mix of fear and pain. Her tears, already streaked down her cheeks, seem to multiply as she clutches her belly, her eyes wide with a desperate urgency.

"My water broke!" she cries out, her voice trembling and full of raw distress. Her hands are shaking, her entire body visibly tense, and I'm caught between the shock of the moment and the overwhelming reality that I did this!

"No, it's too early, your letter said you were due in a few weeks." I panic walking in circles, the elevator closing behind me.

"Knox, go get my bag, it's by the bedroom door."

"It's too early Ana, I fucked it all up! Shit, did I smash him, I was on you! I shouldn't have touched you like that! I was too rough, I sh, "

Ana interrupts my rant, yelling, "Oh fuck, shit, motherfucker, this hurts."

"I'm so sorry, I've been a dad for one fucking second and I'm already fucking terrible at it."

"Knox, do you know how to deliver a baby?" she asks, panting heavy breaths.

"Fuck no, is the baby coming out? I thought it took way longer than that?"

"No, you idiot. But if you don't get your shit together and go get my fucki, Ow, fuck!" She sucks in a deep breath, and between her teeth she continues, "Knox go get my motherfucking bag! Now! I don't want to find out what kind of fucking doctor you can pretend to be!"

I'm frozen for a second, the weight of her words sinking in. The gravity of the situation slams into me, and the world suddenly narrows to just Ana and the urgency of the moment. I rush to her, my own fear blending with a fierce protectiveness, and then I run inside and grab her bag.

March 2

"Tears from eyes worn cold and sad"
-Blink 182

Knox

"**K**NOX, YOU'RE EXHAUSTED, BURNING the candle at both ends. I know this is hard for you, and add the layer of your hate for hospitals, it's too much," my mom says in a long breath. She's literally on the other side of the world, and hearing her voice over the phone is not offering much comfort. Sometimes you just need your mom, here, in the flesh.

"I have been staring at the TV, listening to the same episode of Bluey on repeat. I stare at the TV at home, I stare at the TV in the hospital waiting room, waiting for Ana to wake up. I'm not exactly exerting myself. Mom… when is she going to wake up?" I plead, but the question is rhetorical.

Ana has undergone one of what sounds like will be many surgeries, and is now in a medically induced coma to reduce the pain and stress on her body.

My mom says something, but I'm too tired to focus on her words. I just start rambling, not even sure if it's a logical response to what she just said, not even sure of the significance.

"Mom, I go home at night so Riker can sleep in his bed, and then we get up and head back to the hospital in the morning. I had the neighbor babysit Riker for the first few days while Ana was recovering from surgery. She didn't want him to see her like that. Well, he can't see her anyways, because he's too young to go in the ICU, but he comes here with me anyways. He plays, I stare, and every once in a while he takes a nap on my chest, and I stare some more. We're in a routine."

"Knox, you need rest, and he needs normalcy. You need to take him to daycare."

"There is nothing fucking normal about your mom being in a coma in the goddam ICU! He needs to be here! I need him here. He's my kid!" I yell louder than necessary, making Riker cry. "Shit mom, I'm sorry," I say, shaking my head. "I shouldn't have yelled at you."

"Knox, we will be there tomorrow night. We're coming straight from the airport, our flight leaves at 6:15 am, please, try to get some sleep. I'm worried about you."

This is the worst time for my parents to be in Hawaii. I need them.

"Promise, I had a phone session with my therapist yesterday," I say to reassure her.

I know it's probably not good for a 2 year old to spend his days in a hospital waiting room like this, but he keeps asking about mama, and he can't see her. I don't want him missing both of us all day long.

I'm lost.

Ana will be pissed.

What if something happens? What if she wakes up? He should be here, just in case.

I need to be here just in case.

Ana

I HEAR KNOX AND Riker playing and laughing, but it sounds muffled almost like soft echoes on a video playing. They wave and distort, as if filtered through layers of fog and static, making it hard to grasp the exchange. However, it's a nice break from the tears and painful sounds of Knox's voice as he cries and replays our past like a scratched record on repeat. As this new sound fills the room, it fills my heart.

As I lay here, pain radiates through the right side of my body. It was once sharp and jarring, but has now dulled into a focused persistent ache. The new decreased sensation makes it easier to focus on the sounds around me, and redirect my focus, the sounds of them playing are drifting stronger through the fog of my unconscious state. They are faint but unmistakable and though I can't move or respond, it's a chorus of laughter and playful banter that tugs at my heart. A vivid reminder of the last two years, building a family with Knox. And while it was unconventional and often painful, the joy of Knox and Riker is always pure magic.

As I continue to drift in and out of consciousness, the laughter I hear starts to create a montage of memories from the past two years flooding my mind. It begins with vibrant snapshots of joyful moments.

Laying here in bed, I feel frozen in time, the world outside my consciousness becomes a distant hum, as each memory shifts into a burst of color and emotion, more vivid than any dream I have ever had, as if I'm reliving them in real time, feeling every sensation they bring with them. I find myself drifting off to another time, surrounded by a similar hospital setting with a familiar buzz from surrounding machines.

The hospital room is a sterile, white cocoon, the air thick with the tang of antiseptic. The rhythmic beeping of the heart monitor is relentless, underscoring the sharp, insistent pain pulsing through me with each contraction.

"Just a few more pushes, Ana. You're almost there," the midwife encourages, her voice a calm anchor in the chaos of my labor.

I grip the sides of the bed, my knuckles white, trying to focus on the midwife's face through the waves of pain. Knox stands nearby, his face a ghostly white. He shifts uncomfortably, looking as though he wants to be anywhere but here. This is not how I envisioned bringing our son into the world.

"Knox, come here," I say. reaching my hand out, sweat coating my hand, but he makes no advance to move from where he is standing.

With each contraction, I bare down, pushing with all the strength I can muster. The pain is intense, a deep, primal ache encompassing my entire body. I can hear the encouragement of the nurses, their voices blending into a supportive chorus, but they were quickly drowned out by the sound of Knox breaking his silence.

"I didn't think it would be like this," he mutters, almost to himself. "I'm so sorry."

His voice is a mix of guilt and despair, and his eyes rarely meet mine. I want to reach out, to find some solace in him, but the pain pulls me away from that hope.

"Knox, please. I need you. I can't do this by myself. Please just come here. Hold my hand, please. I'm freaking the fuck out."

He walks over, brushing the hair from my sweat covered forehead. He places my hand gently in his as I feel an urgent sensation… Oh my god I'm going to shit myself.

"Why does it feel like that?" I scream.

"Honey, you're doing great. Just bear down, push like you're trying to poop," the midwife says as if this is the most natural sensation.

My eyes widen and I make awkward eye contact with Knox. "Maybe you should move by my head."

Just then the sensation gets stronger and I feel like I'm being ripped in two.

"Oh fuck!" I yell.

I can feel the stretch of the baby's head, and then the fire of a thousand needles pricking my vag one by one. "What the fuck!"

And then, relief. A sudden, overwhelming sense of relief as our baby enters the world. His cries fill the room, a sharp contrast to the quiet tension preceding them. The midwife quickly places him on my chest, and I feel his warm, slippery body against my skin. Tears stream down my face as I look down at him, this tiny, perfect being I brought into the world. His tiny fingers curl around mine with a fragile grasp. I look up at Knox, hoping for a moment of connection, but he's focused on our son with a melancholy expression.

"He's perfect," I whisper, my voice choking with tears.

Knox's gaze flickers to mine, his eyes softening for just a moment before turning away. "Yeah. He really is."

The next memory invading my mind is our first car ride home. I'm reliving it all over again.

The drive home is filled with an oppressive silence. The streets outside are slick with a recent rain, the sky a muted gray. I sit in the back seat, my hand on the carrier.

Looking at Riker, who is sound asleep, I study every feature. He looks so much like Knox. His nose and mouth are an exact copy of the features I memorized in his daddy. His hair is darker than Knox's, a light brown but has the same small curls at the end. It took Knox and I a few hours to settle on Riker as the name. Knox was insistent he have a strong name. So we did what any parents in need of help do, we turned to google and Tik Tok. We spent hours diving into lists of names, and when I stumbled across Riker, it was a name we both instantly fell in love with. It means a powerful leader. We both agreed he is going to be the one to lead us out of the shit engulfing our life right now. He will be the driving force for all of our future plans and interactions. He will determine how we move forward. Everything will be for him. Riker, our powerful little leader.

My heart lurches, not knowing what tomorrow will bring. I should be over the moon, this should be the best feeling in the world, and the best day of my life. Instead it's covered in a veil of the realization that we are not an "us", it's me and then it's him. Two separate people raising a tiny little human.

"I thought... I thought we'd be a family," I say quietly, my voice trembling. The words hang in the air, heavy with unspoken regrets.

Knox's grip on the steering wheel is tight, his knuckles white. "I didn't expect this either," he replies, his voice flat, strained. He keeps his eyes on the road, avoiding my gaze as if it were too painful to look at me. The last few days have been a whirlwind, and we have not had the time or energy, with all the visitors we had to discuss what happens now, but settled on the fact Riker comes first.

The familiar streets are blurred by the rush of our unspoken disappointment. Each turn seems to deepen the abyss between *us, the promise of a shared future slipping further and further from reach.*

Knox carried Riker's carrier into the apartment for me, and helped me get all of his things settled for our first night at home. We put all of the flowers in vases and set them up around the apartment. We unpacked all of the clothes from the bag and put them in the washer, and put all of the diapers and wipes we got from the hospital neatly in the changing table drawers. Blake and I are on the waitlist for a bigger apartment, but in the meantime, I'd set up a small nook in the corner of my room as a little nursery space.

Settling onto the couch I start to feed my little man. I pull a blanket over the two of us and prop a pillow under the arm holding his head. Riker suckles and I smile down at him. Knox is standing at the blanket closet pulling various sheets and a quilt out, plopping them on the corner of the couch.

"Knox," I sigh. "Go home and get some sleep. You've been sleeping in a chair for two days."

"I'm good," he says as he pulls his phone charger out of his backpack.

"We will be fine. Blake will be home soon and she can help me with anything I need."

"No! I'm the fucking dad! If he needs something, or you need something… it's the first night out of the hospital. No, Ana!" he barks out as he pulls his phone out to send a text, presumably to Mia.

"Do you mind if I invite Mia over? I'll talk to her on the balcony. I have to end things with her. This is not right, and shit

has moved so fast the last few days in the hospital and I havn't been able to really be honest with her, and it's fucking eating me alive. I can't wait any longer to have this conversation," Knox says on a long exhale.

"Knox, you should probably go there. That is not a conversation you invite someone over to have. Especially to the house of the chick who just had your baby," I say.

"Yeah you're right, I'm sorry. I'm tired, and I'm so afraid to leave you alone and I'm not thinking," he says as he shoots off another text. He sits in silence as it dings again, just as the door opens and Blake walks in.

"Told you I was here," she says to Knox.

"Ok, I'll be back in a little bit," he says, reluctant to leave.

He left the room several times to talk to Mia while we were in the hospital. She brought him clothes and a toothbrush so he could stay. As much as I hate to admit it, she's been great these last few days. A gentle hand, steadying the balance. Unseen but always there. She has dropped off food, and run errands for Knox, all while giving us privacy during this time. But most of all I appreciate that I didn't have to see her face. I feel sad for her. She obviously loves him, and I believe he loves her too, but not in the way he should love someone he shares a life with.

Knox is such a good man, and loves so hard. He knows Mia deserves more, and I know lying to her has been eating him up inside, even given the circumstances that have made it impossible to talk to her, be honest with her. But as much as I know he is breaking apart, I admire him doing the right thing and not stringing her along.

As he closes the door behind him, I silently shift my focus back to feeding Riker, eyes getting heavy with each small sucking noise circulating in the air.

Suddenly I'm snapped back to the present, as I hear a loud popping sound. I recognize the laughter of the video Knox must be playing. It's of Riker playing with a balloon on his first birthday. I can picture the scene almost perfectly even though I can't see it.

The living room is awash with a riot of colors, streamers, balloons, and the rich brown of chocolate cake, the center of it all. The room is buzzing with the chatter of guests and the squeals of children.

Both of our parents are here, my brother too. I watch as Ryan plays with Riker on the floor, teasing him with a bright yellow balloon. Riker grabs at it fast, pulling a little too hard at the knot on the end. The balloon pops, the sound echoing in the room. I stand watching, waiting for the tears. I move to go get him, when Knox's hand brushes my arm pulling me back. "He's ok," he says. "Let him figure it out, he's not crying. Let's see how he handles it before we rescue him." Just as Knox finishes his sentence, Riker erupts in the most genuine laughter I have ever heard. He starts handing Ryan one balloon after another making him pop them, until they're all gone. Standing back smiling, I give Knox an appreciative look for stepping in… I love that I get to just watch my brother and son together, bonding and building a relationship. They love each other so much.

Knox and I have fallen into a rhythm, we co-parent well. Knox and I have always agreed when it comes to the important things, never really fighting when it comes to our son. But the distance between us is undeniable. While we have found a grove in co-parenting, the emotional distance gets stronger the more time that passes. Where we used to fall into a natural rhythm, now our interactions are forced and uncomfortable.

"Happy Birthday, Riker!" I call out, my voice filled with joy as he tears into the wrapping paper of his presents. His giggles are infectious, lighting up the room.

"He's really getting big, it's happening so fast," Knox says, as he comes over to help pick up the mess my brother and Riker made, attempting to sound cheerful, but his voice betrays him and I hear a note of sadness. Knox is here almost every day. He stops by on his way home from work, but I know it kills him, not being here for every little moment.

"He is," I manage, forcing a smile through the lump in my throat. "I wish time could slow down."

I glance over and see Knox kiss Riker on the head. The sight hits me harder than I expected, a sharp pang of regret and sadness piercing through the festive atmosphere of Riker's first birthday party.

Despite the joy surrounding me, my heart aches with an unspoken longing. I watch Knox, and I can't help but feel like an outsider in his life. The feeling is a contrast to the happiness I *feel for Riker, and I struggle to reconcile the joy of his milestone with the lingering sorrow of what might have been.*

I'm pulled back to Knox when I hear him and my dad reminiscing about how much Riker loves the fall. I'm instantly transported back to our first outing to the Maple Festival with Riker.

The Maple Festival is in full swing, with stalls lining the streets, each offering a tantalizing array of maple-themed treats. The air is filled with the sweet scent of syrup and the lively hum of festival-goers enjoying the festivities.

Riker, bundled up in a cozy jacket, clutches a small bag of maple candy in his tiny hands. His eyes are wide with wonder as he takes in the vibrant scene around him.

"This place is amazing buddy!" Knox says excitedly, smiling down at Riker. "Look at all the fun things we can do," he says pointing, as if Riker is old enough to understand what Knox is saying to him. I love how Knox interacts with him without ever treating him like a baby. It makes me smile.

Knox walks beside us, his presence a comfortable but charged silence. He's holding a small maple leaf-shaped lollipop, which he offers to Riker.

"Here you go, buddy," Knox says, his voice carrying a touch of warmth.

Riker's eyes light up as he takes the lollipop, his face breaking into a delighted grin.

We wander through the festival, exploring the various stalls and enjoying the lively atmosphere. Knox and I fall into a natural rhythm, our conversation easy and filled with shared laughter. There's a warmth between us that feels almost familiar, yet always just out of reach.

At one point, we stop to watch a group of children performing a dance routine on a makeshift stage. Riker claps his hands excitedly, his gaze fixed on the performers.

"This is so much fun," I say, glancing at Knox. "I'm glad we came together for this, even if it's a little weird being back here."

Knox nods, his eyes lingering on Riker with a mixture of nostalgia and something softer. "Yeah, it's nice. Riker's having a great time."

As we continue to enjoy the festival, I can't shake the bittersweet ache in my chest. The day is filled with moments of joy, but also a lingering sense of what might have been that never seems to waiver, and memories of the last time we were here. Knox's presence is both comforting and painful.

As the festival comes to an end, we head back to the car, I catch Knox's eye. There's an unspoken understanding between us, a silent acknowledgment of the distance that has grown between us, despite the moments of closeness we've shared. Does he still miss me too?

"Thanks for coming today," I say, my voice tinged with a mix of gratitude and melancholy.

Knox offers a small, sad smile. "Anytime, Ana. It was good to be here with you and Riker."

Our conversations have become so calculated. I thought eventually this would get easier, but it's still so hard.

As we drive home, the day's memories linger like a sweet but elusive taste, this was a good day.

Suddenly I have an aching feeling radiating through my chest, and the sensation brings images of the first time Riker stayed at Knox's apartment.

The day feels heavy with the weight of transition. Knox's apartment stands before me, a place that's supposed to be a second home for Riker. I park the car and take a deep breath, trying to steady the nerves twisting in my stomach. I have never been away from Riker.

It's important for Knox and Riker to have their time just like he and I have, but this sucks. I knock, and Knox opens the door almost immediately, his smile warm but tinged with an undercurrent of awkwardness. "Hey, Ana. Riker, come on in, buddy."

"Hi, Knox," I manage to say, my voice tight. "Riker, do you want to show daddy your new toy?"

Riker, clutching a small stuffed fox, holds his arms out for Knox to take him. He loves his daddy.

"Come on, Riker. Let's get you settled in. We've got some cool stuff planned for today," Knox chimes.

As I hand over Riker's small bag, I want to say more, to hold onto him a moment longer, but I force myself to step back.

"You'll be okay," I whisper to Riker, trying to keep my voice steady, more soothing myself than him. "Have a good time."

Knox watches me, his gaze softening with a shared sadness. "He'll be fine, Ana. I'll take good care of him."

"I know, I've just never been away from him," I say, trying to smile through the lump in my throat. "I know he'll be okay."

"Come in," he says softly. We can hang out for a while."

"No, if I come in it will be too hard," I reply, and he doesn't push. He knows what I need.

As I turn to leave, the ache in my chest is almost unbearable. The apartment feels like a reminder of everything that could have been, a family, a shared future. The connection I had with Knox is palpable, an undeniable chemistry lingering like a ghost between us, filling the silence left in the wake of our unfulfilled dreams.

In desperate need of a happier state of mind, I recall more of our happier memories.

Christmas morning dawns clear and bright. The house is a whimsical wonderland of Jack Skellington and Sally, with ornaments hanging from every conceivable surface and the scent of gingerbread and cinnamon filling the air. Knox outdid himself, buying every decoration in the store! Riker's eyes sparkle with anticipation as he bounds into the living room, his pajama-clad feet making excited little pattering sounds on the floor.

"Tanta!" he exclaims, rushing towards the tree.

I smile, my heart swelling at his joy. "Merry Christmas, little man."

Blake went to her parents for Christmas this year to give us some space to navigate our first Christmas together. Last year Riker was so little that he and I went home to my parents. This year, he is so excited about Santa, I wanted Knox to be a part of it. Knox stayed over on the couch and is already in the kitchen, preparing breakfast. He moves with a practiced ease, as if he's done this many times before. After Riker's first Christmas, we promised we would always stay together on Christmas Eve, so we would be together Christmas morning, and neither one of us would miss out on these special memories.

Knox glances over his shoulder, his eyes meeting mine with a mix of warmth and something else, an unspoken understanding. "I thought we could have breakfast together before the gifts," he says, his voice carrying a hint of affection.

"That sounds great," I reply, grateful for the gesture.

We sit down at the table, where Knox has prepared a spread of pancakes, bacon, and fresh fruit. Riker digs into his breakfast with enthusiasm, his face smeared with syrup and joy.

Knox, who has been quiet, finally hands me a small, wrapped gift. "I got this for you," he says, his voice soft and tentative.

Surprised, I take the gift from him, my fingers trembling slightly. I unwrap it to find a simple silver locket. Inside, there's a tiny photo of Riker. My heart catches in my throat as I turn it over in my hands.

"It's beautiful, Knox. Thank you," I say, my voice thick with emotion.

He nods, his eyes softening. "I thought it might be nice to have something to open on Christmas morning, I wanted you to know how much you mean to me and Riker both."

"Knox, I didn't get you anything… I should have, " He cuts me off .

"I didn't get you a gift because I was expecting one. I knew it would make you smile, and I still love that smile," he says.

We sit in comfortable silence as we finish our breakfast.

After breakfast we move to the tree, where we take turns helping Riker open his presents. The room is filled with laughter and the crinkle of wrapping paper. Knox keeps a respectful distance, allowing me to enjoy this moment with Riker, yet I'm so glad he's here with us.

As the morning progresses, I find myself lost in the warmth of the memories we're creating. Knox's quiet support and the unspoken connection between us fill the room with a bittersweet joy.

In the quiet of my comatose state, these memories are vivid and comforting, even the painful parts offer the familiarity I crave right now. Each moment is a tapestry of joy and heartache, a reflection of a life that might have been, how we could have done things differently. But, I hold onto the warmth of these experiences, the laughter and happiness of Riker.

Yesterday, February 28

"Are you afraid of being alone?
Cause I am, I'm lost without you"
-Blink 182

Ana

I fiNALLY SAVED UP enough money to buy a home for Riker to grow up in, well maybe not grow up in, but one he can look back on as his first home with mama. The house is small, in the foothills of Vermont, cozy and inviting, nestled among towering pine trees. Its charming exterior, painted a soft, weathered blue, complements the lush green landscape. Inside, the rooms are modest but cozy, with wooden floors scattered with toys and crumbs from Riker's snacks. The living room, with its stone fireplace, is filled with the cheerful chaos of childhood, toy cars and stuffed animals strewn about. The kitchen, though compact, is functional and filled with the aroma of home-cooked meals. The two bedroom house, adorned with soft linens and a few personal touches, provides a peaceful retreat, just big enough for the two of us.

I'm sitting by the fireplace, savoring the warmth and aroma of my coffee in peace, still hot, not something I get to enjoy often as a mom of an energetic two year old, I can't help but think about how much I love coffee at all times of the day, but especially when it's peaceful and I can savor it. That's when I hear the crunch of gravel outside. Glancing through the window, I see Knox's car pull up outside. It's only been a few hours since he picked up Riker, and the afternoon sun is still casting a golden glow over the landscape, but even more off Knox's dirty blond hair as I see him walking up to the house.

Knox steps into the house, his expression a mix of emotions I haven't seen before. "I forgot Mutton," he says, scratching the back of his neck.

I stand from my seat by the fireplace, setting my coffee cup aside. "Oh ya, that will make your night a living hell if you don't have him. I'll help you look."

Together, we start searching the house, moving through the cozy, but cluttered rooms. As we sift through toys and scattered belongings, I glance at Knox. "Where is Riker now?"

Knox straightens up from looking under the chair, "In the car."

"Knox!" I say with concern as I move towards the front door.

"Relax, Ana, I'm joking," he says with a chuckle. "My mom is taking him to the zoo before they leave for Hawaii on the red eye tonight. I thought I'd come get Mutton before bed time."

I nod, a small smile tugging at my lips. Sometimes there are small moments where we fall into a comfortable groove, giving each other shit, like we used to. "He'll have so much fun. He loves the zoo," I sigh as my heart rate evens back out. "Mutton should be around here somewhere. He's usually in the living room," I say as I continue our hunt.

We move to the living room checking behind cushions and under furniture. Finally, I spot a small tuft of fur sticking out from beneath the couch. "Got him!" I pull out the well loved stuffed fox and hand it to Knox. Our fingers brush lightly, and my stomach curls at the sensation. Knox doesn't pull his hand away, but instead brushes his pinky finger lightly against my hand as he stares down at the burnt orange fur.

It's been so long since there has been any physical interaction between us, this almost feels intimate. I tinge on butterflies circling around in my stomach as I try not to make eye contact with Knox. When he doesn't pull away or stop the connection, my mind starts to whirl, playing tricks on me. He just looks at our hands, rolling his pinky finger up and down the outside of my hand. Up and down, in long slow motions. Over and over again.

"I got a job offer," he whispers, pausing the soft swipes of his fingers and looking up making eye contact for the first time since he's been here. "The Mountaineers want to promote me to an Instant Replay Tech. It's a great pay raise and a huge opportunity."

I look at him with a mix of emotions, feeding off his somber demeanor. "That's great news, Knox. Congratulations."

"Yeah, I just got the phone call. It's a lot of traveling, I guess it's a good thing."

"Oh, this *just* happened. Knox, I could have brought you Mutton, you could have stayed home and processed it all." I search his eyes for something, anything, that might give me a clue about how he is feeling. "It's a lot to take in," I finally say, softly knowing he doesn't need me to point out what he should have done.

Knox nods, his gaze dropping to the stuffed animal in his hand. "Yeah, it is, I just needed a fucking minute you know, to breathe. So I jumped in the car and drove around trying to clear my head, and ended up here. The job, it's a lot of traveling and all I've been thinking since they offered it to me is I need to talk to you. I can't just leave all the time, put extra responsibilities on you. I don't know. I mean, I have a kid with you, we, me and you, have to plan for him first," he says pointing between us.

"Knox, we'll figure it out," I say in my best reassuring tone.

"I'm tired of figuring it out, Ana, I hate my job. It's just a constant reminder of the life I could have fucking had."

"Knox, if you hate what you're doing right now, take the job, you will never regret more money and experience. It's still not ideal, and you will still be watching the game you miss, but the money can help you save for something better. Take the job, and start looking for something else. I work remotely, Riker and I can travel with you if you have a long trip so you can spend time with him and don't have to be away from him for too long. We can think of something else you can do, something to fill that void," I explain. "Just because you take the job doesn't mean it has to be a forever thing, it's never too late to get what you want out of life, Knox. The money could help you eventually open a youth training facility like you've been talking about. Teach kids how to play the game, develop their skills, and learn to love the game again."

He just stares at me with a mixture of admiration and frustration. "How do you do that?" he asks, his voice earnest. "Take a shitty situation and just know how to fucking make it better? This is what you do, you stitch me back up. You know exactly what to say, what I need."

I meet his gaze, a faint smile on my lips. "I don't have all the answers, Knox. I just know your heart."

"What has it been like for you?" he asks.

"What do you mean?" I ask, taken off guard by this abrupt change of topic.

"The past two years, I've never asked you what you've gone through, being a new mom. Things haven't exactly been comfortable between us, so I've never asked."

"Knox, you know my heart too, you know everything about me. You can read me like a book, so you know exactly how it's been for me. So, let's cut the bullshit. What you're really asking is how I've been since it all fell apart, since our fight two years ago we never resolved?"

"I need to hear it from you, I need to hear the words, Ana, so I know I'm not misreading you," he pleads with an urgency I didn't see coming. I'm not sure what's sparking this change, and it takes me a second to catch up to where he has shifted the conversation.

"What words?" I ask as butterflies erupt deep inside me.

"You know my heart, right, that's what you claim? Well then, you know the fucking words I need to hear, don't play dumb, Ana, it doesn't suit you." His voice is low, filled with something resembling desire.

"It's been hard, Knox. One second I had you, we were consumed by each other in a bathroom filled with heat and passion. We'd spent an entire month fucking every chance we could, you were everything I never thought you would be and everything I never knew I needed. I got upset and jumped to conclusions and it set off a chain of events that blew us apart, and before I knew it, you weren't mine anymore, and you were just gone. You were so hurt I couldn't reach you, and it's torn me apart everyday since. I have loved you since the day I met you, Knox, and it hasn't changed. We were a disgusting love at first sight sort of romance, and then you belonged to someone else. When you moved in with Mia, I crumbled inside. I love you so much, Knox. But, I'm not your choice. First you chose her, and then you chose to be alone, and now here we are. We have to figure our shit out, because Riker has us both." I pause, "I just really wanted you to choose me. I love you, Knox, and right now I hate myself for admitting this to you, sounding so desperate. I wanted to date, to move on, but it's impossible with a toddler, and the more time we spent together raising him, the more hopeful I've gotten that maybe you'd fucking choose me," I stifle a sob knowing *"I love you"* are the words he is wanting to hear.

Confirming my suspicions, he springs forward and collides with me, in a heated embrace, our bodies pressing together, with a frantic, unapologetic urgency. This time, there is no hesitation, no pulling away. Knox's arms encircle me, as if he's afraid to let me go. I cling to him, my breath mingling with his in a shared, fervent connection.

He guides me to the couch, laying me down. "I fucking love you, Ana, I always have. I thought you wouldn't want me after the way I handled everything. Trust me, if I believed you were a choice, there wouldn't have been one."

I hear the zipper on his pants as I slowly open my eyes, afraid if I make eye contact, it will all disappear. His erection springs free, a bead of precum glistening in the light of the fire, I can't help but lick my lips at the sight, oh how I missed this. He pulls my sweats down in one fast motion, underwear and all. "Fuck me, Stitch, make me feel something other than this empty ache I feel every time I look at you."

"Knox," I breathe out.

"Don't you fucking dare same my name unless you mean it, unless you are ready to have it fall from your lips in a moan, Anabelle," he whispers in my ear as he tucks my hair behind my ear, causing goosebumps to erupt all over my skin. "I can't take it when I hear it come off your lips."

"Knox," I pant and he places kisses down my neck, nipping the skin in his path.

Just then he flips me over on all fours, rolling his thumb over the tight skin surrounding my hole.

"Knox," I repeat, moving a little out of his reach.

"No, Ana! This ass is mine. This has always been mine! Do you hear me?" With a sexy grin on his face he raises a brow and slowly spits, lubricating my entrance. He lays a soft kiss on my ass, and then runs his finger over my hole again, this time pushing his finger inside.

A soft moan leaves my mouth. With his finger still deep inside me, he uses his free hand to line himself up with my soaked pussy, brushing his thick cock through the wetness, and then slams into me. Hard and fast.

"Oh my god Knox... shit!" I moan.

He doesn't say a word, he just pounds in and out of me, the sounds of skin slapping and heavy breaths filling the silent room. Suddenly he removes his finger, rolling it around the skin surrounding my hole. Then he replaces it with his thumb. The moan leaving my mouth is a sound I have never heard before, and I fall over the edge. Knox pushes into me hard with so much force, I can't catch my breath, moaning his name over and over.

"Your pussy clinches my dick so hard with my thumb in your ass, Ana. It's feels so fucking good!" He slides in and out of me over and over, each time the motion becomes more precise, more intense. He builds speed slamming his dick deep inside, and I can hear just how wet I am. After a few more intense pumps, he gives into his release. Pulling his cock out of my sated pussy, he spills the contents of his release all over my back.

"Fuck, Stitch!" he pants with a heavy breath, "I've never come so fast. It's a little embarrassing," he chuckles. The sound is melodic against the silent room surrounding us.

An hour has passed, and Knox and I are sitting, naked on the living room floor planning out the endeavors of his youth training facility, as he draws little circles on my skin, my head against his shoulder.

Knox shared his vision for the facility, a focus on providing a safe space for at-risk youth, offering support, education, and mentorship while learning baseball. He wants to offer baseball training camps, regular practice sessions for teams, and skill development workshops. His dream facility will feature batting cages, a pitching mound, and a fitness area, with at least one outdoor field for teams to practice. I'm surprised by how much detail is coming out, as if he's been planning this for years and not minutes. His ideas are grand, and the smile on his face warms my heart knowing how bad he wants this and how much it means to him.

This is us, no bullshit, no overthinking, just us, and it feels so right.

Only it's not just us, it's Riker too, but right now in our post orgasm bliss, we are acting as if the complications, the potential fallout of a hook up, doesn't exist. Acting like if we just move on, it will erase everything that has happened.

As we sit and talk, our previous urgency gives way to a comfortable closeness, our conversation flowing freely. But in the back of my mind, I can't help but wonder what this means.

For the past hour, nothing else has mattered, and I let myself live there for a while. But now, the weight of our past, the complexity of this situation slams into my heart.

"Knox, I'm sorry," I interrupt, "I really want to spend all night planning and dreaming with you, but I can't until we talk. What does this mean? You just fucked me, and now we're lying here dreaming of a future, when right now we haven't even decided what 'we' are anymore," I just wait.

After a few minutes he begins to speak, his words careful, precise, and well thought out based on the amount of time he just stared at me. "It means we're finding our way forward. Together. It means after all of this time, we're still us! We're still here, still dreaming, still planning. I've fucking missed you Stitch!"

There is one question I need the answer to before I can move forward. "Knox, why did you move in with Mia?

When we were apart. You loved her, right? Do you miss her? Do you regret kissing me that day, wish it would have never happened? Never blew up your life?" I guess I have more than one question.

They linger in the air. Knox takes a deep breath, his expression thoughtful. "Mia was a big part of my life, and I cared about her. I loved her, Ana, but I realize now I loved her like a best friend. What *we* have," he says motioning between us. "What we've been dreaming up for the past hour, it's about more than just a job, more than a training facility, more than my future. It's our future. The entire time we were talking, I could see it all in plain sight, and every vision was filled with you and Riker by my side through it all. You two are my family, my home. I never had that feeling with Mia, but she taught me love can be patient, and I don't need to lead every interaction with such urgency. She taught me how to be a better man, and I will always love her for that. Everything happens for a reason, Ana, and I needed her to teach me those things so I could be the dad I am today. The man I'm ready to be for you, I just wish I did her right in the process. That's my biggest regret, but one thing became clear the night I came by to see you. It was you then and it is you now. It's always been you, Stitch."

"Then why has it taken us so long to get back here?" I ask, hating how desperate I feel.

"I guess we needed time, well I needed time. I really thought I messed everything up when I kissed you the night you went into labor. I thought there was no way you would want a man like me. I actually went back to therapy and was honest about my struggles after that night, and spent time working on myself. I needed to be a better man for you, for Riker. Then I think we got wrapped up in being new parents. I know I got consumed with being a dad. Time moved so fast, and before I knew it, it had been two years. I didn't know how I was going to get what I truly wanted, *you*." He takes a breath and rakes his hand through his hair, "I'm guessing the same was true for you. It became comfortable and predictable, and with everything changing so fucking fast, I guess I just needed that. After the way everything went down, I didn't know how to make a move for us without fucking it all up, and this time, Riker's happiness was at stake, it's not just about us. It's about him too. I was scared I would rush things, or you wouldn't want me and we'd make it so hard on him. But, fuck, being close to you, and not being able to touch you," he says nipping my neck, "hold you," he whispers, pulling me into him, "only getting to smell the lavender in your hair as you pass me." He lays a soft kiss on my lips, and butterflies erupt. "It gutted me. It's always been you, Anabelle. I've always been yours and you've always been mine. So let's plan our future."

He kisses me again, but this time it's slow and he takes his time.

"I have to go tonight and get Riker from my parents," he says, placing a small kiss on the tip of my nose. "But I just want to sit here with you, just a few more minutes, ok?"

"Deal," I say as I intertwine our fingers.

The time passes and unfolds effortlessly as we just enjoy each other's company. We continue to talk, filling the room with laughter and excitement. The room is lit softly by flickering firelight, creating a cozy nostalgic backdrop.

We share stories and reminisce about our past, our conversation flowing freely as we make up for lost time. We playfully tease each other, filling the space with a sense of ease. Our bond is palpable, marked by gestures of affection and love.

As the minutes tick by, our interactions cocoon us from the world. As it comes time for Knox to leave, the mood shifts slightly, but there is no lingering sadness. We share a deep kiss, a silent acknowledgement of us, and what we want from each other.

Knox stands at the door, ready to head out, his expression a mix of emotions. "I hate that I have to leave, but I'll be back in the morning. Ok?"

"Yeah, okay," I nod.

He turns and kisses me one last time. "I'm going to call Blake and ask her to watch Riker for a few hours tomorrow so we can go for a walk or something, plan what we do from here, how we make sure we figure ourselves out without affecting Riker."

As he leaves, I watch him go, a smile on my face. The night has been truly amazing, and full of possibilities. Yet, I'm nervous about what tomorrow will bring. What does the future look like?

"Tomorrow morning, coffee and orgasms," he promises as he closes the door behind him.

Knox

IT TOOK ME LONGER than I expected to pick up Riker from my parents'. I didn't want to over excite my mom, so I sat keeping my excitement to myself and talked to her for a while about all of their plans in Hawaii. When I dropped Riker off at Blake's this morning I couldn't hold it in, and she was more than excited when I told her why I needed her to watch my boy. Now that Riker is settled with Mutton in the next best place to home, I can finally put all of my energy where I want it.

I hadn't expected Ana to still be thinking Mia was a factor, and when she said she wanted me to pick her, it wrecked me. It's always been her, even when I was fucking everything up, it was her. Having Riker matured me. If it all happened now, I'd handle everything differently, but then I thought I could somehow make everyone happy if I just tried hard enough. I didn't want to hurt anyone, and everywhere I looked, it was painful, destruction for someone. The worst part of it all, was being close to her, and not being able to take her in my arms, hold on to her every time she handed Riker to me.

The first time Riker stayed at my apartment, all I wanted was for her to come inside, I was longing to close the gap between us. So much time had passed, I was unsure how to do that, unsure if she had moved on from her feelings for me, buried them deep in a vault never to be opened. Then as time went on, it felt irresponsible to risk it all. I had a responsibility to Riker not to jump in too fast, to risk the awkwardness of finding out she closed that door. Unsure how we'd move passed it after finally finding a balance. The weight of it all, paralyzing when I could have had her this entire fucking time. If I could go back, I would do it all so differently!

Then, reality struck like lightning, a surge of electricity coursing through me moving me in the only clear direction, back to her. The job offer, the reality of traveling, spending so much time away from her, from Riker, the idea of distance creating an opportunity for her to move on with someone else, was enough to take me under, drown me in the storm brewing inside me. I had no other choice, it's only ever been her. It was time to man up and go for it!

What I didn't anticipate was the conversation bringing up memories of the night I broke up with Mia. It was terrible. I never really processed my feelings about it, because being a new dad took over, so I'm not surprised the memories are resurfacing in detail now, causing emotion. One thing I learned from my therapist is even if feelings seem to come out of nowhere, it's important to process them.

So I do.

I drift back to the night I broke up with Mia.

Reliving the difficulty of the night so I can battle through the feelings it evokes and I can have a clear head when I see Ana.

Fingers trembling, I fumbled with the keys, the metallic jingle echoed in the stillness of the hallway. My heart pounded in my chest as I finally unlocked the door to my apartment, a place that had always felt like a sanctuary but at that moment felt like a motherfucking prison. Every step I took inside was heavy, burdened with the weight of what I was about to do. When I walked out of these doors a few days ago, I had no intention of returning this way. But Ana, shit, she changed everything.

The seconds with Ana unfolded faster than I could calculate. Her presence, her voice, the way she looked at me, all of it stirred something deep inside me, something I'd been trying to suppress for far too fucking long. Before Ana's letter I was happy, ready to start a life with Mia. But when I saw Ana carrying my baby and was finally in her presence after so long, consumed by her, I realized my future didn't belong to Mia.

Somewhere deep down, I think I always knew this moment was coming. Part of me has only ever imagined my future with Ana, even if I couldn't admit it to myself until now. Ana and I… we're like two magnets being pulled together, no matter how much I've tried to push the thought away.

I took a deep breath as I stood in the doorway of the apartment I shared with Mia, about to shatter the life we'd just started to build together. I took another deep breath, trying to steady myself, but it was no use. The guilt was swirling inside me, threatening to paralyze me. But I knew what I had to do. I couldn't lie to her, and I couldn't keep lying to myself.

I took a step further into the apartment, the familiar surroundings suddenly feeling foreign, as if I was seeing them for the first time through a different lens. The couch where we'd spent time curled up together, the kitchen where we'd shared meals and laughter, it all felt like a set piece, a facade about to come crashing down to the fucking ground.

Mia was in the living room, scrolling through her phone, completely unaware of the shit show about to hit. She looked up as I walked in, a forced smile tugged at the corners of her lips with the faintest eye roll. It was the kind of reaction from her that usually stirred up an argument. I could tell she was annoyed I'd been distant and not let her be a part of the last few days, it made my chest tighten with guilt.

"Finally, you're home," she said on a long exhale. Her voice was relieved and a little annoyed, even though I could tell she was trying her hardest to hide it.

"Hey," I managed to reply, my voice shaking. I hesitated, the words I needed to say stuck in my throat like jagged stones. How do you tell someone you're leaving them? How do you break someone's heart when they've done nothing wrong, but done everything right?

I took a deep breath, forcing the words out before I could lose my nerve. "Mia, we need to talk."

Her already fragile smile faltered, a flicker of concern crossed her face. "What?" she asked, I assume picking up on my intention.

I looked at her, the woman who has cared for me, supported me, loved me, and I felt a deep ache in my chest. But I knew what I had to do, what I wanted to do. I couldn't keep living this lie, couldn't keep pretending my heart belonged to her when it had been with Ana all along.

Deciding it was best just to get it out, I started, "Mia, I can't do this anymore, I kissed Ana." My words were heavy, final.

Her eyes widened in shock, her breath catching in her throat. "What the fuck, Knox?" she asked, her voice trembling.

"I… I can't do this anymore," I said, my voice cracked. "I'm sorry, FUCK!" I yelled, hitting my head against my hand as if it would make the words hurt her less. "I'm sorry. I'm not mad at you. I'm mad at myself. I told you I didn't know what would happen, but being with you was what I wanted, and I did. I did so badly, but when I saw her-I have a family Mia. I have to focus on being a dad, and I lost control and kissed her, and you deserve better than that." I knew my words were abrupt and scattered, but it was all I had. The silence that followed was paralyzing. Mia stared at me, her eyes filled with tears, the reality of my words sinking in. I wanted to reach out, to comfort her, but I knew it was too late. The damage was done.

"I never meant to hurt you, please know hurting you was never my intention, this isn't fair to you," I whispered, my heart

breaking as I watched her crumble before me. "I can't stay here when I'm clearly in love with Ana, we have Riker, and that's where I belong, whatever it looks like."

Tears spilled down her cheeks, and she turned away, unable to look at me. "When? Today? You kissed her today?"

" No, right before she went into labor. We got in a fight and, " She cut me off.

"Just go," she said, her voice choked with emotion. "I don't want the details."

I hesitated, wanting to say something more, anything to make this right. But I knew there's nothing I could say to ease the pain I'd caused her. So I turned and walked to our room and packed a bag.

After throwing everything in a bag and walking towards the door I looked at her, pain lacing her eyes. "You can stay here if you want, I'll move out," I said, knowing this was not the time for this conversation, but not knowing what else to say.

"I'm not staying here, Knox. I'll go to my parents' house. I'll be gone by the weekend. You were barely together, Knox, and she turned her back on you at the first sign of trouble in your relationship. You know what, forget it. If this is how you feel, it's not worth the argument. Get the fuck out so I can pack. You made me look like a fool for days. You kissed her and then let me come there and bring you shit." She didn't look at me, and I couldn't blame her. I was such a prick. As I slowly walked out of the apartment, I heard her quiet sobs and it killed me. The door closed behind me with a thud that echoed in the emptiness of the hallway.

As I walked away, the weight of what I'd done crashed down on me, but I knew there's no other way ... man, it felt like shit.

Today, March 1

"So here I am, I'm trying
So here I am, are you ready?"
-Blink 182

Ana

THE EARLY MORNING LIGHT filters through the curtains, casting a soft, muted glow over the room. I'm pacing the length of the small living room, my hands clasped tightly around a coffee mug that's gone cold. Each step feels like a step closer to a moment I've been hoping for. The silence of the house is punctuated only by the soft shuffle of my feet and the occasional clink of the mug against the coffee table.

I glance at the clock on the wall for what feels like the hundredth time. Time seems to stretch and contract with each passing minute, making the wait un-fucking-bearable. My heart is pounding, a mix of anxiety and hope clawing at my insides. I want to relax, but the anticipation of seeing him again is making it hard.

The door creaks open, and I freeze in my tracks, butterflies erupting in my stomach. Knox stands there, his eyes heavy with exhaustion, his face drawn and pale. There's a look in his eyes I can't quite decipher, something between sadness and resignation. I feel a pang of anxiety and a rush of concern as I take in his disheveled appearance.

He changed his mind.

His shoulders slump slightly, as though he's carrying the weight of the world on them.

"Knox," I say softly, my voice trembling slightly despite my efforts to keep it steady. "What's wrong?"

He steps inside, closing the door behind him with a soft thud. His eyes meet mine, and for a moment, the silence between us is thick with unspoken words. "Our conversation last night sparked memories of when I broke things off with Mia, and how badly I handled everything. I never really processed all of it. Time got away from me with being a new dad, and I, I just feel like such a piece of shit. I was such a tool back then," he finally says, his voice low and strained.

I watch as he moves towards the couch, sinking into it heavily, his body seeming to give in to the exhaustion and emotional toll of the morning. The cold coffee on the table seems like an afterthought now, and I can't help but feel a pang of sadness for what transpired for him last night.

"I'm so sorry, Knox," I say, my voice barely above a whisper. I sit down next to him, reaching out to place a comforting hand on his arm. "I didn't mean to resurface old shit. You are a good man, we got caught up in the moment, we were young. It wasn't right but you did the right thing by being honest and letting her go."

I pause and a sinking feeling settles into the pit of my stomach. "Knox," I say, clearing my throat. "Do you remember the first time I came to your apartment?"

"Of course, that night was amazing. Every teenager's dream comes true, only we are adults," he laughs.

"I never said anything because I didn't think anything of it then, but you had a bottle of whiskey out on the table when I got there, then some time later you told me about the pills you had in your pocket the night we met." My words fall off, and I pause again.

"Yeah, that was a long time ago, what's wrong?" He asks as he pulls me into him. "Why are you thinking about that right now?"

"Are you ok? Like right now, you are really down, and I want to make sure you are not… I don't know how to ask this," I say, but he rescues me.

"Baby, look at me," he says using the hook of his finger to bring my eyes up to his. "I invested a lot of time in myself, doing the work. I'm still doing the work. Getting to a better version of myself for you and Riker. Do I still struggle, yes. Do I still have moments where cravings set in, yes. But, baby I am in such a different place now. I have a purpose I lost when I got hurt. I have strategies, a tool box I didn't have then." He places a kiss on my lips. "I promise, there are no pills in my pocket, I don't even have them at home, and I appreciate you checking on me and facing it head-on. I need that."

"I believe you, I'm sorry."

His eyes close briefly, and he takes a deep breath, as though trying to gather his thoughts and emotions. "Don't be sorry, Stitch. You are perfect, you didn't do anything wrong. I just… I didn't realize how much it would hurt, thinking about it again, picturing the hurt in Mia's eyes all over again. It's like every decision I've fumbled in some way."

"Breaking up with someone is never easy, Knox. Someone always gets hurt," I reply not knowing what else to say.

Knox looks at me, his eyes reflecting a mixture of gratitude and weariness. "Thank you for waiting for me all night," he says.

I squeeze his arm gently, offering a reassuring smile. "Where was I going to go? You promised me we'd start the day with coffee and an orgasm. You know I'm a sucker for starting my day that way," I wink, trying to lighten the mood.

He smiles. "I can't wait, but I need to clear my head first. Can we go for that walk and talk about us?" he asks.

"Yeah, let me go get changed," I say as I push off the couch.

I'm standing in front of the full-length mirror, the soft hum of the heater in the background providing a comforting backdrop to the early morning stillness. This is not the first time I've found myself looking at myself in the mirror contemplating my future with Knox. Apparently, this is where my thinking happens when it comes to him. I pull on a pair of warm, comfortable leggings and a cozy hoodie, the fabric soft against my skin. The weather outside promises a crisp, invigorating walk, and I want to be ready for it, both physically and emotionally.

I glance at the clock, it's early, and Knox and I need this walk to clear our heads and talk. The past few hours have been a whirlwind of emotions and changes, and the quiet morning seems like the perfect opportunity to figure out what we do next.

As I slip into my favorite pair of converse, I let my thoughts drift to Knox. Despite Knox's emotional strain, I feel so hopeful about today. I've been looking forward to this walk since last night when he mentioned it, not just for the fresh air, but for the chance to share some space with him.

I finish adjusting my laces and grab a lightweight jacket, the kind that's perfect for chilly mornings but still breathable. I take one last look in the mirror, giving myself a small, encouraging smile.

As I step into the living room, I see Knox by the door, coffees in hand and looking as if he's ready for a change of pace.

"Ready?" I ask, slipping on my jacket and zipping it up. My voice is light, matching the hopeful energy consuming me.

Knox looks at me, a loving smile tugging at his lips. "Yeah, ready," he replies, nodding.

I can't help but notice the warmth in his gaze as he looks at me, and I offer him a sexy little smile in return. We both need this, both the walk and the time together to talk about our future.

"Let me just put my phone on the charger, I was on it all night trying to distract myself until you came back," I say, plugging it in and placing it on the table by the front door.

We step out into the crisp morning air, the world outside still wrapped in a gentle quiet. I take a deep breath, the fresh air filling my lungs. I feel a sense of calm settle over me. I have missed him so much.

As we walk, our steps fall into a comfortable rhythm. We talk about the future, about our hopes and fears, and about finding a way through the challenges inevitably lying ahead as we truly become a family. We wander aimlessly through the walking paths surrounding my house, everything else blurring into the background as our focus remains solely on each other. The challenges of turning two lives into one appear less daunting as we dissect them. We realize this transition can be as simple as we make it, and for Riker, it won't affect him much at all.

As we talk, the conversation between us flows effortlessly as expected.

"Let's go pick up Riker and get ice cream. Oh, and we can go look for Halloween decorations," I say excitedly.

"The house is a little bigger than the apartment so we need more stuff."

"How many decorations do you need?" he laughs, "Are there really any you don't have?"

"Knox, new decorations come out every year, you just don't want to go shopping."

"That is correct, I hate shopping. Plus I highly doubt you've gotten any more efficient over the years, I bet you still wander aimlessly up and down every aisle over and over. You turn a 20 minute shopping trip into an all day event."

"Are you saying you don't want to spend time with me? Even if it is walking behind me through the store," I joke.

"Baby, I'll spend all my time behind you," he says, wiggling his brows.

As the sun rises higher and the world awakens, with families scurrying around us on their walks, people passing by us on their morning runs, or walking their dogs. I feel relieved to finally have my Knox back with me where he belongs. And in this moment, walking beside him, I feel a glimmer of hope for what lies ahead.

As we walk it feels almost like a dream, almost too perfect to believe.

We're on our way back, approaching the house, so close to home, when the tranquility is abruptly shattered.

Out of nowhere, a motorcycle roars into view, its engine loud and aggressive against the peaceful morning.

The rider takes the corner too sharply, and my heart skips a beat as I realize the bike is heading straight for us.

My instincts kick in, and I immediately move closer to Knox, standing closest to the street, but the bike's trajectory is too unpredictable. Before I can fully react, the motorcycle skids between us, pushing Knox into the street and there's a blinding flash of metal and motion.

Everything happens in an instant. The bike crashes into me, the impact sending a jarring shock through my body. I feel a sharp, searing pain as I'm thrown off balance, and the next thing I know, I'm hitting the ground with a force that knocks the wind out of me.

The world around me spins, the sounds of the motorcycle slamming into something fades into the background as a piercing pain surges through me. I hear Knox's frantic shout, but it's distant, muffled by the haze of pain and confusion.

I try to move, but my body feels heavy and unresponsive. I'm lying on the cold pavement, and the world is a blend of colors and shapes. Tears of pain and shock cloud my vision as I struggle to comprehend what's happening. My breath comes in short, ragged gasps, and I can barely make sense of the voices around me.

Knox is by my side in an instant, his hands reaching for me, his voice laced with fear and concern. I can feel his presence, his warmth, but everything else is a chaotic jumble. His touch is both reassuring and terrifying, as if grounding me to reality even while I'm overwhelmed by pain.

"Ana, stay with me! Can you hear me?" Knox's voice cuts through, full of a desperation that tugs at my heart.

I try to respond, but the pain makes it hard to focus. My limbs feel numb, and I can barely move. My thoughts are a tangled mess, and all I can do is try to hold on to Knox's voice, his touch. The world around me is a swirl of faces and sounds, and the pain is all-consuming.

In the midst of it all, I find myself desperately wishing for everything to stop spinning, for the pain to ease, for Knox to stay by my side. I want to tell him I'm okay, that I'll be alright, but the words are trapped in my throat. All I can do is cling to the hope of knowing he's here, he'll help me through this, and somehow, we'll find our way back to the quiet, serene morning we had just moments ago.

I can feel the blood seeping through my clothes and down to my fingers. My vision blurs and I fight to stay conscious, the world around me becomes a mix of sounds and colors.

Knox is beside me, his face showing panic and fury. "Motherfucker!" he yells, his voice raw with desperation. He fumbles his phone, only to realize it's dead. He lets out another string of curses. "FUCK! I didn't take a fucking charger when I left last night!" I hear.

I try again to speak to him, to tell him I am ok, but words don't come. My breaths become shallow, each inhale a struggle. Knox looks at me, wild with fear, and I can see him calculating his next move.

"I'm going to get your phone," he says, his voice urgent and shaky. "Stay with me, Ana. Fucking hold on, ok!" His feet pound against the pavement as he runs towards the front door.

I can hear the faint sound of Knox, tearing through the house. The minutes stretch into eternity, each second a battle to stay conscious. Finally I hear Knox burst back out the front door, phone in hand. He kneels down beside me, already on the phone with 911, hands trembling as he brushes the hair soaked in blood from my face. "They're on the way Ana!"

He repeats himself yelling it louder, "They're on their way!" But I realize he is yelling to a few people who appear to be tending to the motorcycle driver.

I try so hard to focus on Knox, I try to stay with him, but I just can't. I'm so tired, so cold, I just can't. I watch his face disappear in a swirl of black engulfing my vision as everything fades to black.

Knox

"ANA, NO, NO, NO, come on baby just open your eyes." I'm not sure how many times I repeat myself, chanting in a continuous loop. "Ana, baby please. This can't be the end, this can't be the end of us. I just got you back, please."

"Sir," I hear, but I can't bring myself to respond. "Sir, I need you to come with me so we can get some information.

"Ana, do you remember the day we met?" I whisper to her, it's all I can do to ground myself, so I talk to her.

"Sir."

"No, I have to be with her."

"Sir, you'll be in the way. She is losing a lot of blood, and they need to focus on what they are doing without interruption or interference," he says calmly. "Can you tell me her name, and age?"

"Huh?" I ask.

He repeats himself, "Her name and age."

"Ana, Anabelle Scott. She's um, she's 26."

"Do you remember what happened?"

"It just fucking happened, of course I remember!" I snap. "We were walking, I was going to tell her I loved her and wanted to move in with her, and a motherfucking douchebag who had no fucking business being on a bike, ran her the fuck over."

"Ok," he says, seeming a little annoyed at my tone. "I want you to go sit in the back of the ambulance while they check her out, and I'll keep you updated."

Numb, I do what he says. And before I know it I'm sitting in the ambulance being checked over by one of the paramedics. My heart is pounding because I can't see her. Straining, I ask, "Have you heard anything?" Then without warning, in a flash of panic, they slide her inside the ambulance. She's strapped to the gurney, covered in blood. They move at lightning speed to secure her in and then take off. Everything whirling by in a slow flash. I move, sitting by her head and just holding her hand. As I rub her small hand in mine, my mind wanders as they rattle off her injuries.

Broken clavicle.

Shattered wrist.

Shallow breathing

Possible punctured lung.

Blood loss.

Laceration over her right eye.

Broken fingers.

Laceration on left arm.

Possible broken hip or pelvis.

The list seems to go on forever, and I'm numb. I can't feel anything, I can't focus on anything, except her face. This is not the serene kind of numbness that comes from being with her, where all of my problems disappear, or the numb abyss that comes from the aftershock of two small pills sliding down your throat. No, this is a numbness born from sheer fucking self preservation, when your body slithers inside itself holding on to any shred of hope to protect your mind, your heart from being obliterated as you watch the love of your life hang on for dear life. At least that's how it feels. It feels like she's dying.

"Knox, he can't see me like this. Riker can't see me like this," she chokes out.

"Ok," I say, snapping my eyes down to meet her gaze, wiping the tears from my face. She's right here, but she feels a million miles away.

"Please, Knox, tell him how much I love him."

"Ana, baby calm down. It's ok. He's with Blake." I try to reassure her.

She closes her eyes, and I rub her hand, brush the hair from her face, and just whisper in her ear. I tell her I love her and she's going to be okay. She is in and out of consciousness the entire ride to the hospital.

"Where is Riker?" she asks each time she regains consciousness.

"RIKER!" she shouts and writhes on the gurney as they give her medication to calm her down.

"Our first date was amazing, Do you remember, baby?" I ask, trying to distract her.

She doesn't answer.

"You walked into The Pit and slid in the seat next to me, and I swear my fucking heart stopped," I begin to relay the detailed memories flashing through my mind.

They pull her out of the ambulance and rush her inside while someone escorts me to the emergency waiting room.

I collapse into the chair, and put my head in my hands still covered in Ana's blood, and cry. I fucking cry. I don't know for how long, because today every second feels like an eternity. I'm not even sure how we fucking got here. I should have held her a little tighter in our hug, or taken her to bed when she made her flirty little advance to lighten the mood. I should have driven to the house a little slower, or faster for that matter. Just a few seconds, is all we needed. A few seconds of being distracted or rushing out of the house a few seconds sooner in more of a hurry, either one and we would have missed this shit show all together. It's bullshit, when you think about it, that one carefree decision as small as plugging your phone into the charger, or looking into those blue eyes a few seconds longer, can change the entire trajectory of the day. A few seconds, and she wouldn't be here fighting for her life, we would still be at home planning our future together.

"Mr. Reed, the paramedics said you came in with Anabelle Scott," the doctor says as he moves towards me in the waiting room.

"Yes," I respond as I push out of my chair.

"Come with me, I'll fill you in on our walk upstairs."

"She's already in a room? Is she ok?" I blurt out and eagerly await his response.

"No, we're going up to the surgical waiting room. Ana experienced some pretty significant injuries. Some of them we were able to address in the ER, but she is going to need a few surgeries in the upcoming days. We were able to stop most of the external bleeding and secure her wounds enough to then be closed in the OR. She lost a substantial amount of blood, so they will provide her with a transfusion during the surgery. We took her in immediately for a CT, and she has a small bleed in her brain from the impact of the fall, but it will likely resolve itself, as it was minimal. However, before we address the extent of her injuries to her limbs, we have to repair her lung, and get any further internal bleeding under control. Which is why she is being prepped for surgery now, the sooner we get in there the better."

"Can I see her?" I plead.

"I'm afraid not. She is in a great deal of pain so we have her sedated and we need to get her into surgery as soon as possible. We will keep you updated."

"And the motorcycle driver?" I ask, unsure of what I want to hear.

"We lost him." With that, he turned toward the double doors at the back of the waiting room and pushed through them.

Fuck, that can't be Ana's fate too. She has to be ok. I need her to be ok.

I sat for four hours and waited. Ana's parents and brother arrived shortly after the doctor left, and when Blake arrived with Riker, I was relieved. Honestly the distraction he offers is the only thing saving me right now. We have gotten a few updates through the cell phone they provided, but they are minimal. All we really know right now is while she is considered critical, she is stable for now. They were able to repair her lung, but are having a hard time getting some of the internal bleeding to stop. It's controlled, but it has not been alleviated.

So we wait.

Another hour passes, and she is out of surgery and has been moved to recovery. Everything went as good as could be expected, but they will have to put her in a medically induced coma to help control the pain. Her body was having a trauma response and led to a seizure in post op. Because of this, they have her sedated to help her body heal, and hopefully avoid any additional seizures.

March 4

"Do I have to die to hear you miss me?
Do I have to die to hear you say goodbye?
I don't wanna act like there's tomorrow"
-Blink 182

Knox

I SIT IN THE uncomfortable plastic chair of the hospital waiting room for the third day in a row, my eyes darting between the clock on the wall and the small figure beside me. Riker squirms restlessly, clutching Mutton tightly. My parents stopped by Ana's on the way here to pack Riker a bag of toys and snacks. They look exhausted from their back to back flights. It took them a while to get back, but man, I'm glad they're here. I don't know what I would do without them!

The sterile scent of antiseptic fills the air, mingling with the faint sounds of beeping machines and murmured conversations. I can tell Riker is getting tired, needing a nap. I'll call Blake to come get him so he can nap at home where he's comfortable.

He looks up at me with wide, curious eyes, sensing the tension but too young to understand its source. I try to muster a reassuring smile for him, though my mind is elsewhere, consumed with worry for Ana. I know her mother is with her in the hospital room, offering what comfort she can. This is just a fucking disaster!

Why the fuck did I insist we take a walk? Who in their right mind needs to clear their mind before sex? Sex clears your fucking mind!

These thoughts invade my mind and I watch Riker continue to squirm around. "Let's go get some food, buddy," I say to him as I pick him up. We walk over to the nurse station before we leave the ICU waiting area. "We're going downstairs, I have my cell if anything changes," I tell the nurse, I don't bother telling her which patient I am referring to, she already knows.

She nods. "Mr. Reed, enjoy some time away, she will be just fine. Mrs. Scott is with her, and she is stable." She tries to reassure me that getting out of here is a good idea.

They tried to wake her yesterday morning, but her body is still under too much stress. They reduced the sedative and her blood pressure started to rise along with her heart rate. They're hoping this new pain medication will create more relief and will make it easier for her body to transition off all the sedatives. They'll try again tomorrow morning.

Every time the doors to the ICU swing open, my heart leaps. The minutes stretch into what feels like hours as I wait, the uncertainty gnawing at me. I gently stroke Riker's hair, silently willing myself to calm the fuck down.

My mom took Riker home for the night. I slept in Ana's room on the recliner in the corner, so her mom could have the sofa bed by the window. I didn't get much sleep, I was too anxious about the thought of them trying to wake her up again this morning. It's 7:30 now, and her mom went to grab us both a coffee, so I'm passing the time by playing old videos for Ana, of Riker, hoping his laughter reaches her.

"Hi, Knox," the doctor says as he walks in the room and places hand sanitizer in his hands from the small dispenser by the door.

"Hey, Doc. Ana's mom ran down a few minutes ago to grab us coffee, is it cool if we wait for her?" I ask.

"That will be fine, I'll check her vitals while we wait."

A few minutes pass and her mom returns with two coffees in hand, sleep deprivation taking over her strikingly beautiful appearance. While Ana favors her father's dark appearance, her eyes and smile come from her mother. Today, the slight dark circles adorning her eyes, a trait Ana inherited, are slightly more pronounced. I cannot imagine how hard this is on her seeing her daughter like this.

"Ok," the doctor breaks his silence as he takes a seat in the rolling chair near the end of Ana's bed. "Ana's vitals are stable, and her labs look great. In about 30 minutes, the anesthesiologist will come in and start to reduce the sedation. If she tolerates the pain and all of her vitals remain stable, we will continue this for the next few hours. It could take her up to 24 hours to start showing signs of consciousness. However, it may take several days for the signs of consciousness to be visible. We are fairly confident she is in a good space right now, and this will be successful. Before we discuss what to expect, do you have any questions?"

Ana's mom rattles off a few questions to include the surgeries she still needs to repair the broken bones, but I cannot for the life of me focus on anything she is asking. I'm not sure what I would do if I was here alone right now. My brain can't register anything other than the internal strum of my racing heart.

She's going to fucking wake up!

"Knox, do you have any questions?"

The doctor interrupts my thoughts, bringing me back to reality.

I shake my head, "No, not right now"

"Alright," he continues. "This is going to be a long and difficult process. The first signs of consciousness will be responses to simple cues such as light and sound. After some time, she will become more alert, but will be very confused, agitated, and seem delirious at times. This will be the hardest stage of regaining consciousness to watch. It will feel like she is taking steps backward but I can assure you she's not. Even though it will be hard to watch, everything you will likely see is normal. Eventually she will transition to the final stage of recovery where she will become more alert, and respond without difficulty. She will no longer be delirious, but may still have a hard time with problem solving, judgment, and decision-making."

I know what the doctor said, and I know he knows what he is talking about, but holy shit, this is no joke. I sit beside Ana's bed, my heart in my throat as I watch her face for any sign of life. Each day in this hospital drags on, a painful blend of hope and dread. I've been here for what feels like an eternity, each second a slow torment. The beeping of the monitors and the soft hum of the machines become a haunting background to my thoughts. I cling to the smallest signs of movement, the faint twitch of her fingers, a slight shift in her eyelids, anything that might indicate she's beginning to come back to us.

The doctors tell me it's a good sign, her brain is responding, her vitals are stable. But it's a cold comfort when I'm sitting here waiting, feeling completely helpless. The agony of seeing her so still, and so disconnected from the world, eats away at me. I'm trapped in this limbo where hope feels like a cruel joke, and my own emotions are full of fear and desperation. Each time her eyes flutter open, only to close again, my heart skips a beat, torn between the thrill of possibility and the crushing disappointment of it fading away.

I keep talking to her, pouring my heart out in whispers and gentle touches, hoping my voice might pierce through the fog that's keeping her from me. The anguish of waiting is unbearable, each moment of her being unresponsive feels like a heavy weight pressing down on me. I don't know how much longer I can fucking do this! I want so desperately to see her smile again, to hear her voice, to see her beautiful blue eyes and to know she's truly back with us.

The room is quiet except for the steady rhythm of the machines and my own ragged breaths. I sit clutching Ana's hand, my eyes locked on her face. Suddenly, there's a shift, a subtle change. Her eyelids flutter, then part slightly, and I can barely believe it. I lean in closer, my heart racing with a wild mix of hope and fear. I sit up straight and scoot to the edge of my chair.

"Ana?" I whisper, my voice trembling. Her eyes open a fraction more, and for a fleeting moment, there's a glimmer of recognition. It's like I'm seeing her through a veil, and I want to reach through and pull her back fully. I squeeze her hand, feeling a weak response, a faint pressure. "Ana, can you hear me baby?" I ask softly.

Her breathing starts to quicken, and my hope spikes. But then, it happens, her body tenses, and her eyes widen in alarm. There's a sudden, erratic beeping from the machines. My pulse pounds in my ears as I watch her struggle, her movements jerky and chaotic. Her chest heaves, and I see fear and panic in her eyes.

I call for the nurse, my voice breaking as I try to keep my own fear at bay. The room erupts into frantic activity as medical staff rush in, pushing me aside with practiced efficiency. I watch helplessly, my hands trembling as I see Ana's body writhing on the bed. The alarms grow louder, more insistent. The doctors are shouting instructions, their faces set in grim determination.

In the midst of the chaos, Ana's eyes meet mine one last time, filled with confusion and a heartbreaking vulnerability. Then, her breathing falters, and the beeping of the machines becomes a frantic crescendo. I'm left standing at the edge of the storm, my heart in my throat, as the room spins with all the urgent activity.

"We need you to wait outside," the nurse demands without any emotion, ushering me towards the door, and closing it, slamming it in my face, my heart plummeting with exaggerated force.

"Stitch!" I gasp, tears pouring down my face.

March 8

"I miss you, took time, but I admit it"
-Blink 182

Ana

I'M DRIFTING IN AND out of darkness, caught in a fog that feels both heavy and suffocating. Everything is murky, and I can't make sense of it. My body feels alien, and there's a dull ache everywhere. Then, suddenly, there's a burst of clarity. I'm aware of my surroundings, but it's disorienting. My eyes open to a room full of bright lights and faces and they all seem to melt together.

I try to move, but my limbs feel like lead. I'm confused as I struggle to piece together what's happening, a rush of anger floods through me. Why am I here? Where is everyone? I try to speak, but my voice comes out raspy and weak, a mere whisper against the backdrop of beeping machines and muffled voices.

Everything is too loud, too bright. I don't understand why they're all staring at me like that. I feel trapped, like I'm being held down by invisible chains. My frustration mounts as I try to make sense of the chaos around me. "What's happening?" I want to scream, but it comes out as a hoarse croak. "Why am I here?" I start to panic.

The faces crowding around me, nurses, doctors, family, seem foreign. I feel a surge of rage at their intrusion. Why can't they just leave me alone? My thoughts are a jumble, and the simple fact they're trying to help only seems to enrage me more. I lash out with whatever energy I can muster, trying to push them away, feeling like a caged animal fighting for its freedom.

My emotions are all over the place, confusion, fear, anger. I want to cry, to shout, to demand answers, but my body betrays me. The anger I feel is overwhelming, an uncontrollable force making me lash out at anyone within reach. I don't know what's happening, or why I'm here. All I know is I want to escape from this strange, invasive world that's forcing itself on me.

"Riker, where is Riker?" I can't make out the response echoing around me.

Suddenly I feel two sturdy hands wrap around my face.

"Baby, can you hear me? Anabelle. Baby, please just take a breath please."

With all the strength I can muster, I slowly take a breath. There he is, my Knox. I take another long breath. He slowly starts to climb in the bed with me but the nurse reaches out to stop him.

"She's a little agitated right, " Knox puts a hand up, cutting her off.

"It's fine. She just needs a minute to catch up." He continues to climb in next to me, laying on his side. He presses his face to my profile and whispers in my ear, peppering small gentle kisses to my temple as he slowly rubs my head. "It's ok, Stitch. You came back."

"Where did I go?"

"Too fucking far, baby," he says, gently moving my face towards his and placing a slow kiss to my lips. "You got hurt, but they're fixing you up, you've been asleep for a while, but it's taken a few days for you to fully wake back up. You scared the shit out of me two days ago, but now…" he trails off and I can tell he's choking back a sob. He never cries, he's strong. But right now I can tell he's not.

"Knox, where is Riker? Is he okay? Is he scared?"

"He's been here almost everyday. He hasn't seen you yet, he asks about you, but no, babe, he has no idea what's going on. He's not scared, he's okay. They said you can see him later. Just rest right now."

"Knox, he, "

"Shhh." He cuts me off with his finger placed gently on my lips to silence me. "Just rest, Doc's orders, or they'll make us leave." I turn my head slightly to look over Knox's shoulder, and see Ryan and my parents standing not far behind him, tears rolling down their faces.

I don't want them to go, so I do as Knox says and rest my head back. Trying hard to fight it, but my body wins, and sleep starts to pull me in.

The healing process is a journey unfolding gradually, piece by piece, like a mosaic being painstakingly assembled. It begins with the initial chaos of waking up from a coma, a disorienting, jarring experience where everything feels foreign and overwhelming. As the days pass, the intensity of those first moments starts to ebb, and the process of recovery starts to take shape.

At first, everything is a struggle. My body is weak, and simple tasks feel Herculean. The physical therapy sessions are grueling, each movement a challenge as I work to regain strength and coordination. My muscles ache from the effort, and every small victory, raising an arm, taking a step, feels monumental. It is only compounded by the restriction from unresolved injuries. I have a shattered wrist. They put a temporary plate in until I am strong enough for another surgery, and I'm in a walking cast because my ankle is fractured.

Mentally, it's no less taxing. My thoughts are fragmented, and the process of piecing together memories and understanding what has happened to me is both frustrating and exhausting. The confusion of waking up in a world that has moved on without me makes it hard to focus, and I grapple with the emotional toll of being thrust back into reality. To make matters worse, I have only been able to see Riker via FaceTime because they won't let him in here.

The support of those around me, family, friends, and medical staff, becomes a crucial lifeline. Their encouragement and patience provide a source of comfort and motivation. But the realization that Knox is here, really HERE with me, is what is getting me through. I slowly begin to trust their presence, allowing their reassurance to temper my anger and frustration. Conversations become a vital part of my healing, helping me reorient myself and find a new normal.

As time goes on, the anger fades, and is replaced by a determination to recover. I have to see my baby. Riker is my driving force. I start to embrace the small improvements, celebrating each achievement as a step toward regaining control over my life. The sessions with physical and occupational therapists become less daunting and more like collaborative efforts to rebuild my strength and skills.

Emotional healing is a slower, more complex process. I work through feelings of vulnerability, fear, and uncertainty with the help of counseling and support groups. I begin to understand that healing is not just about physical recovery but also about coming to terms with the psychological impact of what I've been through.

Gradually, the sense of normalcy begins to return. The world around me starts to make sense again, and I find myself reintegrating into my life with a renewed perspective. The healing process is not a linear path but a series of steps forward, setbacks, and moments of profound realization. Through it all, I learn to appreciate the resilience of the human spirit and the importance of embracing each moment of progress, however small it may be.

The transition from the ICU to a regular room feels surreal. My body is still fragile, and every movement is tinged with a mixture of relief and exhaustion. The sterile, impersonal environment of the ICU gives way to a room that feels almost like home, decorated with calming colors and personal touches. The constant beeping and hissing of machines are replaced by a quieter, more serene atmosphere.

I'm still in a daze, my emotions raw and unfiltered. The staff carefully move me, and I catch glimpses of the world outside my hospital room, the corridor, the sunlight filtering through windows. It's all so overwhelming. I'm still trying to piece together the fragments of my life, and my heart pounds with anticipation and anxiety.

Then, Knox walks in, his face a mix of hope and concern. He's holding something, or rather, someone, in his arms. My breath catches as I recognize the small, familiar face peeking up from his shoulder. It's Riker. He's holding Mutton, his favorite little fox, and his eyes are wide with curiosity and a bit of shyness.

The moment our eyes meet, a wave of emotion crashes over me. The sight of him, so small and innocent, brings a flood of tears. I reach out with trembling hands, and

Knox gently places Riker in my lap. The weight of him is both grounding and surreal. I feel his tiny arms wrap around my neck, his warm breath on my cheek. I close my eyes, overwhelmed by a mix of joy, relief, and an intense, indescribable love.

Riker's face is full of wonder as he looks up at me, and I can see he's sensing something momentous but doesn't quite understand it all. I'm choked up, unable to find words, my voice breaking as I whisper his name. I press my face against his, feeling the softness of his skin, and the sweetness of his scent. My tears fall freely, a mix of happiness and an aching sadness for the time lost.

Knox stands beside us, his presence a comforting anchor. I can see the relief in his eyes as he watches this reunion unfold. His hand rests gently on my shoulder, a silent promise and reminder he is here.

The moments stretch out. It's as if the world narrows to just the three of us, this fragile, tender space where love and healing intertwine. Every touch, every small gesture, every shared glance is a reminder of the strength and beauty of our bond.

Knox moves Riker to the couch by the window and sets him up on the iPad. The change of pace in the moment is abrupt as he ignores my pleas to keep Riker in bed with me, he hovers, his face is covered in emotions, his eyes darting between us and the window, where the late afternoon light filters in.

He paces for a moment, clearly agitated, his fingers tapping nervously against the door frame. Finally, he takes a deep breath and strides over to me, his face set with a determined, almost desperate look.

"Ana," he says, his voice low but intense. He leans in close, making sure I can see the urgency in his eyes. "I need to talk to you, now."

I nod, my heart pounding. Riker is engrossed in the cartoon, his laughter filling the room with a joyful, contagious sound. I missed it so much.

Knox doesn't waste any time, he's clearly got something on his mind and he needs to get it out. He grips my hand firmly, his gaze unwavering. "Look," he starts, his voice cracking with emotion, "I know this is probably the worst timing possible, but, " He takes another breath, and I see him gather every ounce of courage he has. "Ana, I need you to marry me. Right now. I know this is, well, insane, but I can't wait any longer. We have been through too much shit, you waited for me for two fucking years, I took forever to accept my feelings, and then you almost fucking died. I thought you died, baby, and I had lost you, just when I finally got you back. Time fucking hates us, the universe hates us, so I can't wait. I want us to be together, I *need* us to be together, to get through this shit, whatever happens. I want you back in my life fully, and I want to be in yours, forever. I don't want to spend another minute without you as my wife,

Stitch. You, my only fucking craving is you, it's always been you, please marry me."

His words tumble out in a rush, raw, unfiltered, and full of feeling. There's no pretense, no romantic flourish, just the urgency of someone who's been through hell and can't imagine facing the future without the person they love by their side. He's sweating, his eyes wide, almost pleading.

I'm stunned, my emotions a whirlwind as I process his urgent declaration. The gravity of his words, combined with the overwhelming relief of seeing him and Riker, makes my heart swell and ache. I see the sincerity in his eyes, the desperation, and the fierce love he's pouring out in this moment. The whole room seems to hold its breath, the clamor of the outside world falling away as we stand at this precipice together.

Knox's confession hangs in the air, love and desperation. The moment feels suspended in time, and I'm left grappling with the overwhelming reality of his words, my heart torn between the rush of emotions in this moment and the daunting road ahead.

One Year Later

"How could I ever forget layin' in your bed?
Having sex all night, it's fucking with my head
Now we can never pretend that we can only be friends"
-Blink 182

Knox

IT'S BEEN A WHIRLWIND year to say the least. The hospital room where Ana and I had an urgent, raw conversation feels like a memory now. We've come such a long way since then, but the journey hasn't been easy. We've had to rebuild, our lives, our relationship, our sense of normalcy, but here we are, on the brink of something new and truly amazing.

As we sit together at the kitchen table, surrounded by piles of wedding magazines and color swatches, there's a buzz of excitement in the air. Ana's eyes light up with every new idea, and I can see the joy in her face as she discusses flowers, dresses, caterers, cakes and venues. I think the trauma of everything that happened changed her outlook on all the "girly" things a wedding entails, or maybe it just made her simply appreciate the idea that she is here, and we are getting married like it has for me. Her enthusiasm is infectious, and I can't help but smile at how far we've come. It feels surreal to be planning this day, given everything we've been through, but it also feels so right.

I watch her flipping through the pages of the bridal magazine, her fingers tracing over pictures of simple gowns and colorful floral arrangements. She looks so content, so at ease, and it makes my heart swell. It's a stark contrast to the fear and uncertainty we faced just a year ago. There's a sense of normalcy now, a feeling that despite everything, we've found our footing again.

"Do you think this color would work?" Ana asks, holding up a swatch of deep navy blue. I nod, trying to focus on the details even though my mind keeps drifting back to how lucky I feel. This wedding isn't just a celebration of our love; it's a testament to our resilience, and our determination to build something, despite all of the chaos of our past.

"Knox, we're actually doing this!" she says for what seems like the hundredth time, as if she is trying to convince herself this is real. Her words ground me, and I look at her with a renewed sense of purpose. I know that despite the hardships, we've built something so unbelievably strong. Our love has been tested in so many unimaginable ways, and it has prevailed through it all. Now, as we plan our future together, the wait is pure torture. If it was up to me, I would have been married right there in the hospital room, no big ceremony, no white dress and tux, just the three of us.

We finish up our planning for the day, and as I look at Ana, she amazes me. She's been my rock, my source of strength, and she has pieced me back together one small stitch at a time. She made me a dad, and she gave me purpose when I felt like I had none.

As we get Riker ready for bed, and give him a bath, I pull her close, resting my chin on top of her head. The weight of the past year, its struggles and triumphs, feels lighter when I'm with her. Our wedding day will be a celebration not just of us really becoming a family, but of everything we've overcome. And as we move forward, I know that no matter what challenges lie ahead, we'll face them together, stronger than ever.

The kitchen is a mess, with crumbs dusting the countertops and the rich aroma of lavender mingling in the air. Ana and I are knee-deep in the chaotic joy that is wedding planning, and today's adventure is a cake tasting.

Ana stands at the kitchen counter, carefully arranging a pile of cards full of cake flavors and descriptions from her favorite bakery, her eyes twinkling with a mix of seriousness and flirtatiousness. "Alright, let's go see if these cakes live up to the hype," she says, her voice teasing. She leans to grab her purse, giving me an excellent view of the way her jeans hug her curves.

I raise an eyebrow and playfully reply, "I'm more interested in how well these cakes compare to the taste of my future wife."

She laughs, the sound light and inviting. "Oh, is that so? Well, you might just have to taste-test me later to make sure I'm the one."

I grin, leaning in close as I pick up the keys and lean in and lick her neck. "Mmm, not too bad," I say, eyes locked on her, savoring both the smell of her shampoo and the taste of her skin.

Ana's cheeks flush slightly, and she playfully nudges me. "Careful, or I might start thinking you're just saying that to get in my pants."

I laugh, enjoying the flirtatious banter. "Would it be so wrong if I was? I'm definitely looking for ways to sweeten the deal. I bet the taste of your pussy on my tongue would make the frosting taste like a completely different treat."

"We're going to be late," she teases as she pushes past me towards the garage door.

When we arrive at the bakery, the tension between us is hot. We spent the entire drive over pushing each other's threshold just a little bit further with every small touch, every kiss, and dirty whisper. With every bite of cake Ana takes, watching her lick the frosting from her lips and let out a soft moan when she tastes one she likes, my dick swells in my pants, making it hard to focus on the task at hand: picking a motherfucking flavor.

As she reaches for another slice, our hands brush together, and the contact sends a jolt straight to my cock. Her playful smirk grows, and she leans in, whispering,

"Well, if you're going to keep flirting like that, I might just have to fuck you right now."

The cake tasting becomes a delicious game of flirty challenges. We playfully compete to see who can come up with the best description of each cake, filling them with subtle innuendos and our laughter fills the room. Who knew cake tasting could be so fun.

"I really love the lemon, Knox, it's firm and exciting in my mouth. I feel like it's really unexpected," Ana says with a soft moan as she swallows the small bite of cake, and then runs her tongue along her lips in a slow sensual motion.

We finally settled on the champagne cake with raspberry filling, a decadent choice that seemed to perfectly blend flavors, and Ana's description sold me, "Mmm. Knox, this is so delicious," she'd whispered. "It has a soft wet center that feels so good in my mouth, smooth and warm, and when it combines with the creamy frosting, it just feels so right."

When we leave the cake shop, I grab a box containing a little bit of leftovers of our chosen cake flavor. It rests comfortably in my hands. I catch Ana's eye, and a mischievous grin spreads across my face.

"You didn't have enough cake?" she asks, playfully.

"You know," I say, giving her a sideways glance as we head toward the car. "I have a little idea."

Her curiosity is piqued, and she raises an eyebrow. "Oh yeah? What kind of idea?"

I open the car door for her and, as she gets in, I set the box carefully on the back seat. "Well," I begin, sliding into the driver's seat and turning to face her, "I'm thinking we should have a little more fun with this cake. You know, really make sure it's as perfect as we imagined."

She looks at me, a mix of amusement and intrigue lighting up her face. "And how exactly do you propose we do that?"

I lean in closer, my voice dropping to a playful, seductive whisper. "How about we take this slice home, get cozy in bed, and make it a tasting experience of our own? I'm thinking the cake might taste even better if we sample it in a… different setting."

Ana's eyes widen, and she bites her lip, clearly tempted by the idea. "You're too fucking much," she says, but there's a hint of excitement in her voice. "But, you might be onto something."

We make our way back home, and as soon as we're inside, I set the cake box on the kitchen counter and turn to Ana with a grin. "I want you on my face."

I carefully cut a generous slice of the cake and place it on a plate. Ana watches with a playful sparkle in her eyes as I lead the way to the bedroom. The anticipation between us is palpable, and when I lean in to kiss her, I snake my hand between her legs, groaning when I feel the seam of her jeans soaked through.

She strips down to her panties and climbs in bed, and I set the plate on the nightstand. When I climb in next to her, she presses her body close. I feed her the first bite, and she accentuates the bite with a seductive lick of her lips. Her eyes close briefly in pleasure, and she lets out a soft moan instantly making my dick rock hard. I slowly kiss down her body, stopping at her wrist and laying slow kisses over the intricate scars covering her skin. I lay sensual kisses over each scar I pass as I worship her body. Her strength is buried in each scar, especially the marks adorning her stomach from our son, and they drive me absolutely wild. She is the strongest person I know. I lean over and place another piece of cake between my fingers and slowly bring it to her mouth.

"Mmm, this is incredible," she murmurs, looking up at me with a mixture of satisfaction and desire. "But I think it would taste even better with a little more… flavor." With that she slowly unzips my pants and pulls them down slightly, my cock springing free. She dips her finger in the frosting and runs it up the sensitive ridge at the front of my cock. She follows it with slow long passes of her tongue, making sure to add just a little more pressure with each pass of her tongue.

"Fuck," I moan.

I pull her up, and lean in to steal a kiss before offering her another bite. "You wanna taste?" she asks, as she lowers her middle finger between her legs, making a quick pass between the wet lips of her pussy and then uses it to scoop a small piece of frosting off the cake. She then takes her frosting coated finger and gently slides it in my mouth.

"That's the best fucking frosting I've ever had."

"Yeah? You want a little bit more?" she asks.

"No." I flip her over and run my teeth along the curve of her ass, making soft bites all the way up her back. She pants and writhes beneath my touch, and I'm fucking here for every second of it. The small moans, and twitches of her body only turn me on more. I lean down and nip her earlobe as I slide a finger in her warm wet pussy. One finger turns into two, and then three.

"Knox, please!"

With her desperate cries filling the room, only accompanied by the sound of her arousal on my fingers, I pick up the pace, making a slight come hither motion with each pass of my fingers. Just as she is about to come I pull my fingers out and flip her over. "No," she pants, "keep going."

"I told you baby, I wanted you on my fucking face." I reposition us so I am on my back and she is riding my face reverse cowgirl. I slowly bury my tongue inside her as she leans down, and swipes her fingers through a piece of frosting that fell on the bed next to us. She then leans forward laying the frosting in a long line down the ridge of my cock, following it with her tongue. Before I know it, the tip of my dick is slamming into the back of her throat. She is hollowing out her cheeks as she sucks me in hard while slowly gliding me out of her mouth at the same time. I instantly feel like I'm going to come down her throat. Before she can take me fully in her mouth again I lift her off me, laying her down beside me as I climb over her again.

"You're going to come on my dick!" I command as I line myself up and push into her just as her walls clench around me. She instantly comes with a vice grip on my cock. I move in and out, trying hard to pick up my pace with each thrust working against the friction of her orgasm. She closes her eyes and moans. Another orgasm building. I reach out and squeeze her chin between my fingers, making her eyes meet mine. "If you wanna come again, you fucking look at me while you do it." The words barely finish leaving my lips as she screams her release, and I follow, sweaty and completely sated.

The Wedding Day

"Yeah, we're doing it all night long"
-Blink 182

Ana

As I STAND IN front of the mirror, the reflection that greets me is both thrilling and surreal. The dress I've chosen is everything I wanted: sexy and simple, yet elegant in its own understated way. It's a sleek sheath of ivory satin that hugs my figure perfectly, accentuating every curve without being overwhelming. The design is minimal, just a smooth, unadorned bodice with a subtle plunge and a high slit revealing a hint of leg with each step.

The soft, flattering fabric feels luxurious against my skin, and the way it skims over my body makes me feel both confident and a little daring. The plunging neckline adds a touch of sultriness, but it's done in a tasteful way still feeling appropriate for the occasion. The simplicity of the dress is its strength, highlighting my natural features and allowing my own sense of style to shine through. The dress shows off more of my scars than I wanted, but given how much Knox worships them every time we're together, I felt it was important to show some off, and be proud the way he is. Plus, I think Knox being able to see them might actually turn him on.

This dress is a stark contrast to the only other dress I wore for Knox. The memories of the seductive yet loving exchange float through my mind. While I am 100 percent positive Knox will be peeling this dress off me later, it will not be because he knows I am uncomfortable in it. I know Knox, and he will be plotting his move all night, making his intentions perfectly clear to only me, through soft whispers of filthy promises to come.

As I turn slowly, admiring the way the dress moves with me, I notice how the light catches the fabric, giving it a soft, ethereal glow. The fitted silhouette makes me feel like I'm wrapped in a beautiful, delicate secret, and I can't help but feel a thrill of excitement at how it accentuates my every move.

The dress is paired with a pair of strappy, nude heels adding just the right amount of sex and class. My makeup is understated but flawless, enhancing my features without overshadowing them, and my hair is styled in soft waves and is tied back in a simple low ponytail styled updo. I've kept my jewelry simple, just a pair of delicate earrings and a bracelet to match, so as not to compete with the dress's clean lines.

The room is filled with the gentle hum of activity, my bridesmaid and maid of honor, Blake, flitting about, adjusting my sleek short train and offering words of encouragement as the photographer snaps a photo of me sitting on the chair pretending to fasten my strap on my shoe. "You look stunning, Ana. Knox is going to lose his shit when he sees you!" Blake says as she steps back and beams at me. "Oh! And fuck me, did you see Knox's old teammate Cash? Holy shit, he's so hot!" Her excitement is controlled, but I can't wait to tell Knox to hook them up.

"I'll be sure to pass the message on to Knox," I chuckle as my thoughts drift.

The air is thick with the scent of fresh flowers, lavender, per Knox's request, and the occasional burst of laughter from our moms visiting in the corner of the bridal suite, but beneath it all, my heart is pounding with a mixture of nerves and exhilaration.

Passing by the mirror one last time, I catch glimpses of the woman I've become, an open book for those closest to me, hopeful, and ready to step into a new chapter of my life. My hands are slightly trembling as I adjust the delicate bracelet Knox gave me, a silver cuff bangle-simple and clean on the outside, but filthily engraved on the inside. A hidden message just for me: I love fucking you… I mean, I fucking love you.

I can't help but replay the moments leading up to this day, the laughter, the planning, the unexpected sexcapades with cake. The journey we've been on has been anything but ordinary, and there is a lot I would change if I could do it all over. For me, the growth we made in our time apart has made us better parents for Riker, and better versions of ourselves for each other. Our wedding day feels like a beautiful culmination of our shared experiences, our shed skin, and our new chapter.

The nerves hit me again as I think about walking down the aisle. What if I trip? What if I forget my vows? I glance around at the three women in this room with me, their smiles a reassuring reminder of the support and love surrounding me. I take a deep breath, focusing on the joy rather than the jitters.

In the midst of all the chaos, Knox's face comes to mind. I remember the look he gave me the first time we met, the overconfidence he oozed when he bit down on his lip ring, his fuckboy attitude almost kept our paths from merging. Then I think of the day at The Pit, and the first glimpse I got at the real Knox Reed. He's been my rock through this last year, and the thought of seeing him waiting for me at the altar makes my heart race and my core heat. The idea of exchanging vows with him, of promising to stand by his side for the rest of our lives, fills me with something I can't quite put into words.

As the final touches are added, my dress is secured, and the last few strands of hair are adjusted, I take a moment to close my eyes and savor the feelings swirling inside me. There's a thrill of anticipation, a deep-seated happiness making every anxious thought feel insignificant in comparison. This is the day we've been waiting for.

When the time comes to walk down the aisle, I feel a flutter of nerves combined with an overwhelming wave of excitement. I link arms with my brother, my heart pounding as the doors open and the soft strains of our chosen song begin to play. Ryan has been the best male role model in my life with unwavering love and devotion, so asking him to walk me down the aisle felt like the only choice. Each step feels like a journey toward a new beginning, and as I get my first glimpse of Knox standing at the altar, his eyes locked on mine, I know everything we've been through has led us to this perfect moment. I look down and see Riker flicking at a button on his jacket, standing next to his daddy. My two handsome men are waiting for me, and the walk to them seems so far, I feel the urge to quicken my pace to get to them quicker, but am brought back to the moment as I feel my brother tug back on my arm slightly reminding me to slow down.

Then the world narrows to just him and me, and as I continue making my way toward him, every nervous flutter in my stomach is replaced by a deep, unwavering sense of trust and love.

Knox

S TANDING AT THE ALTAR, Ethan by my side, I try to keep my nerves in check as the guests settle into their seats. I'm not sure what I'd do without him and Ryan. Even though Ethan moved, he's been a consistent place to lay my emotions through everything that's happened, only a phone call away. Ryan stepped up to help with Riker as Ana healed and we planned today.

The ceremony is about to begin, and despite all the planning, my mind is a jumbled mess. Then, the doors at the end of the aisle open, and my breath catches in my throat.

There she is. Stitch.

She steps into view, and for a moment, the world around me disappears and it's just her. My heart pounds in my chest as I take in the sight of her. The dress hugs her body like it was made for her, every curve accentuated making my pulse race, and my dick stir to life. We had a little pep talk about him refraining from making an appearance today, but apparently he's silently telling me to fuck off. Clasping my hands together in front of my embarrassing display, I watch her intently. The sleek satin gleams under the lights, clinging to her figure with a perfect blend of elegance and raw sex.

Her neckline plunges in a way that's both tasteful and tempting, giving just enough of a hint to drive me wild. The high slit in her dress reveals a glimpse of her leg with each step she takes, and I can't help but imagine what it would be like to touch, to feel her smooth skin beneath my fingers. The way she moves is both graceful and provocative, and my mind instantly drifts to thoughts decidedly less appropriate for a wedding.

I see the way her dress flows around her as she walks, each step making it shift and shimmer. My gaze locks onto her, unable to look away as she gets closer. The anticipation is almost unbearable, and I can't help but let out a soft, almost primal groan as I imagine how stunning she looks up close.

When our eyes meet, I can see the playful glint in her eyes, and it sends a shiver down my spine. The smile on her lips is both sweet and mischievous, she knows exactly what kind of effect she's having on me. It's a look that says she's ready to celebrate not just our love with the people in this room, but a promise for a private celebration later.

My attention is diverted by Riker's antics. He's bouncing on his toes, trying to peek over the edge of the chairs in front of him, his tiny fingers reaching out as if to grab the moment and make it his own. Every so often, he lets out an excited squeal, his voice carrying through the quiet room.

"Daddy, look! Look!" he says, pointing excitedly in Ana's direction, his voice echoing just a bit too loudly in the hushed room. I try to shush him gently, but it's no use, he's too caught up in the excitement of the day to be quiet.

I glance at Ana, my heart skipping a beat as she approaches, chuckling at Riker. Despite my overwhelming emotions, I can't help but smile at Riker's unrestrained joy. He's clearly having a blast, completely oblivious to the formality of the occasion. He's twisting and turning, his eyes darting around, his excitement making it hard for me to focus solely on her.

When Ana finally reaches us, Riker's gaze locks onto her, and he immediately tugs at my arm, trying to get a better view. He's practically bouncing in place, his little face lit up with awe and pure, infectious happiness. As Ana stands next to me, Riker's hand slips into mine, and he looks up at her with a bright, eager grin.

"Hi, Mommy!" he chirps, waving his free hand with enthusiastic admiration. Ana's face softens into the most radiant smile, her eyes shining with love and affection, and she bends down to give him the biggest kiss. The sight of them together, her in her stunning dress, and him in his tiny suit, is pure perfection.

Throughout the ceremony, Riker remains a lively, charming presence. He occasionally lets out giggles, tries to grab a flower from a nearby arrangement, and even attempts to mimic the officiant's gestures, much to the amusement of everyone around us. His playful interruptions and curious nature add a lighthearted touch to the proceedings, making the day feel even more special and filled with joy.

Every time I glance down at him, I'm reminded of how far we've come and how much our little family means to me. The ceremony, though filled with its own formalities, is beautifully punctuated by Riker's exuberance, making it a day that's uniquely ours, filled with love, laughter, and the unfiltered joy of a three-year-old who's experiencing it all for the first time.

When the time comes for our vows, my mom approaches the altar, pulling Riker towards her seat to sit on her lap.

"Ana," I exhale. "When I met you, I was a shell of myself, and you quickly put me back together. You are more than I could have ever deemed myself worthy, and I know what life is like without you, and frankly I'm not interested. You are it for me, you and Riker are my world. If I get nothing else in my life, I already have everything."

Ana smiles, a small tear sliding down her cheek, "Knox, fate and time are not on our side, ever. The timing and structure of our relationship has been chaotic and messy, and everything I never knew I wanted. We can live our lives like Jack and Sally, make messes in the kitchen, and just be unapologetically us every single day. But one thing I know for sure is I can't ever make the mistake of waiting again. Riker and I might be your whole world now, but we are going to have to expand the circle just a little bit to fit one more." My eyes widen and a wide beaming smile fills my face.

"I'm pregnant, and I'm due in seven months."

The reception is in full swing, a vibrant celebration with guests mingling, dancing, and enjoying the festive atmosphere. The guest list is small, Ana really wanted an intimate setting, and I'm so glad we kept it small.

"Knox!" I hear from across the room.

"Cash, I'm so glad you made it!" I say grabbing his left hand in mine and pulling him in for a hug with my right. "I hear the maid of honor has been digging on you all night. You should go say hi!"

"The redhead? Fuck yeah, I will!"

Cash and I talk for a bit and then I make my way back over to my wife. The room is adorned with soft lighting and casts a romantic glow over the scene. With Riker happily at home with a sitter, we paid a little extra to come pick him up and stay the night, Ana and I have been granted the freedom to focus on each other.

Ana looks stunning in her dress, sleek, sensual, and perfectly-fitted. Every time she moves, the dress highlights her curves, driving me wild. As the night unfolds, our conversations start to drift from casual chatter about how perfect everything is, to a more suggestive and flirtatious tone.

We find ourselves at a quieter corner of the reception, our drinks in hand, but our attention solely on each other. The buzz of the party fades into the background as we lean in close, the intimacy of our conversation growing with every word.

Ana's eyes lock onto mine, one hand on my chest and her voice lowering to a sultry whisper. "You know, it's been such a perfect night, but I can't help but think about how much more fun we are going to have once we get out of here."

I can't help but smile at her suggestive tone. "Oh? And what kind of fun are you talking about?"

She shifts slightly, her dress moving in a way that accentuates her every curve. "Well," she says, her voice playful, "let's just say I've been daydreaming about tonight. And I'm looking forward to spending some quality time alone with my husband."

I raise an eyebrow, feeling a thrill at her words. "Sounds intriguing. What did you have in mind?"

Ana's fingers lightly graze my arm, her touch sending a shiver through me. "Let's just say this dress has been driving me nuts all night, because I'm not wearing anything underneath."

My pulse quickens at her words. "Fuck me."

Her lips curl into a teasing smile. "Exactly. Fuck me, Knox."

I grab her hand and quickly pull her out of the room and into the nearby coat closet. Pushing her against the door so it can't be opened, my cock strains against my pants. Just like every time we check our resolve at the door, our motions are rapid and clumsy. Our hands are everywhere, pulling and clawing at each other with frantic need. Ana looked like a stunning vision of grace all night, but there's no way in hell she's making it out of here with the same elegance.

I quickly unzip her dress and chase it to the floor, craving the smell of her arousal in the air around me. On my knees in front of her I pepper small kisses to her slightly swollen belly, still a little soft from Rikers grand entrance into the world. Then I quickly focus my attention on the small silver balls decorating her clit, that shine like jewels dripping promise in the soft glow of the lamp in the corner of the small room. With one swipe of my tongue, Ana shivers and lets out a small moan.

"Knox, fuck me."

"Anabelle Reed, what the fuck have I told you about saying my name like that?"

"Cut the domineering bullshit and fuck me, Knox, before you waste our time."

"Anabelle, we have all the fucking time in the world!" I promise as I place a kiss on one of the scars on her arm, a reminder of how precious time really is. The thought ignites my desire for time to slow down, anchoring into what little control I can, I slow my pace and kiss every inch of her body, taking my fucking time as I worship my wife.

Curious what fate has in store for Blake and Cash? Turn the Page to read the first chapter of This Time Around.

This Time Around

Prologue

"**F**UCK, YES! RIGHT THERE, don't stop, don't stop Cash."

I chant his name over and over in my mind as Cash Easton fucks me, the force barreling into me, making contact with the perfect spot deep inside me with each thrust. He just might actually have the largest dick I have ever encountered and holy shit, does he know how to use it? When he pulls out of me, laying slow kisses down my body, an unwelcome emptiness replaces the full sensation I was adjusting to. The hollow void lingers in the air with a palpable absence, as though something vital has been torn away.

"No, what are you doing?" I ask, disappointed as he lowers me to my back.

A slow roll of his tongue over my clit, and I have my answer.

Since the age of 15, some have characterized me as being more on the promiscuous side, engaging in sexual exploration. I would say I'm comfortable with my sexuality. One time was all it took. The intensity of every sensation being heightened as an orgasm builds within me is electrifying. I decided then that feeling like I needed to justify my desire for orgasms was a waste of time. Besides, the only people with strong thoughts about it are usually those who aren't getting any anyway.

I love sex. So right now, I am completely content with the fact that I only met Cash a few hours ago. As I gaze down at him through lust coated eyes, buried between my legs, his mouth glistening with my arousal, I want nothing else but him.

"Bend over so I can watch your fine fucking ass bounce, Blake." He demands as he sits up, placing all his weight on his heels as he leans back. "I want to see every fucking inch of your body." Without question, I pull myself onto all fours on the bed in my hotel room. I prop my arms on the headboard and arch my back, just far enough so I know every inch is on display. I even give it a little wiggle for good measure, and the moan spilling from his lips is pure sex. A devilish grin spreads across my lips.

"I want you back inside me," I pant, peeking over my shoulder.

"I want to play with your ass," Cash whispers in my ear as he runs his hands over the swell of each cheek.

His request makes me pause a moment, surprised by this boldness. "How about you fuck my pussy? It's nice and wet." Again, I wiggle my ass in his direction. I know a lot of guys love ass play, and in the right setting, I'm all for it. But tonight, after a long day at the wedding, with a stranger, no thanks.

He doesn't argue; he doesn't push the issue; instead, he slides down between my legs and goes back to working my pussy with his magical tongue. He lays slow strokes of his tongue across my clit as he licks it from behind, and before he can quickens the pace, he slips me onto my back again. Cash is gorgeous, and I'm not sure if it's the alcohol or just the way he is, but he is indecisive as hell in bed, moving positions at rapid fire. I send up a prayer for the former because he's too pretty to be bad in bed.

Is Cash bad in bed?

No sooner does the question occur to me, he glides a finger inside me, making an upward turn with his finger. Instantly locating my g-spot as if he's memorized its precise location. My toes curl and just as the pressure builds in my core, he takes his other hand and gently pushes down on my stomach right above my pelvic bone. The sensation has me reeling; "Fuck, Cash. Oh, my god!" It sends a wave of warmth surging through my body, electrifying every nerve. It pulses with a thrilling intensity, almost too powerful to contain. The sensation builds, rich, flooding my senses with a rush of euphoria which feels all-consuming, as though time momentarily suspends. As he adds another finger and begins pumping them in and out of my drenched pussy, each touch and each breath amplifies the feeling, sending shivers like a tidal wave from my core outward, leaving a lingering blissful tremor echoing long after my peak.

Holy fuck, well, he just answered my question.

Breathless and panting, I barely have enough strength in me to wrap my legs, which feel like jello around Cash's waist as he lines himself up, and slides inside of me. His motions start off unhurried, pumping his hips back and forth as he wanes directions, making small circular motions with his hips, pushing his cock to an overwhelming depth within me. His motions increase as he approaches his release.

"Fuck, Blake." He growls as I feel his cock swell inside me. His whole body shakes as he empties himself. We lay here for a few seconds, both catching our breath.

During the elevator ride up from Knox and Ana's reception, we agreed this was a one-night thing, with no strings attached. Cash lives in San Diego, so we won't see each other once he goes home; no sense in catching feelings for no reason, right?

So when he got right up, removed his condom, and threw it in the trash can by the TV, I shouldn't have felt a twinge of disappointment, right? And when he picked up his shoes after he threw on his pants and shirt, not even bothering to button it, and walked out of my hotel room with a wave and a half-ass goodbye, it shouldn't have stung. But it did. It fucking stung like hell. It cheapens this night between us, and even though sex is not something I usually fuss over, and I've had my fair share of one-night stands, right now I feel a little used. I genuinely thought we had something here; at least it felt like we did. I guess in the back of my mind, I believed that all the flirting we did while dancing was creating a connection. We had chemistry. Or I thought we had chemistry. I also had a tiny little hopeful thought in the dark corner of my mind- maybe after we had sex, it would light a fire to the connection, and he would stay after realizing how good we could be. We would spend the night tangled in the sheets. Then, in the soft glow of the sun peeking through the curtains, we would decide to get breakfast. Our conversation would shift to both of us, deciding we wanted to see each other again, and we would sip our coffee and discuss how we could make this all work.

How could I be so dumb? So naïve? Guys don't fall for their one-night stand, ever.

After I washed my face and brushed my teeth, I sat down on the edge of the bed as a foreign sensation set in.

Shame: she is a sneaky, ugly bitch!

Finish Reading This Time Around

Want more of Ana and Knox?
Preorder the Christmas Novella, This Christmas,
on Amazon and Kindle Unlimited.

Acknowledgements

I WOULD LIKE TO express my deepest gratitude to my family for their unwavering support throughout this journey. To my husband, who endured late nights and countless revisions without a single complaint, I literally could not have done this without his love and support.

A special thanks to my sister in law, Alyssa, for believing in this story and championing it tirelessly. Brooke, Amanda Jean, Aimee, and Lindsey also deserve special love for their insightful feedback and dedication to shaping this manuscript, and supporting my journey as a new author! You were the best Beta readers, and sounding board I could have ever asked for.

Heartfelt thanks to my mama and daddy. It's not every day your baby writes smut, but you support it like it's the best thing ever!

This book would not be the same without the exceptional copy editing by JJ Boehs, you helped me really bring my story to life.

Finally, to the readers who embark on this adventure with me, thank you for giving these characters a home in your imagination.

www.ingramcontent.com/pod-product-compliance
Lightning Source LLC
Chambersburg PA
CBHW020245010826
48973CB00006B/1659